The Kissing Ball
A Regency Christmas
And Other Short Stories

By
GL Robinson

©GL Robinson 2020-21. All Rights Reserved.

As always, in memory of my dear sister, Francine, who loved Christmas.

With thanks to my Beta Readers, who always tell me what they think. And with special thanks to CS for his patient editing and technical help.

Cover Art: GL Robinson. Designed with Midjourney, 2023

For a FREE short story please go to my website:

https://romancenovelsbyglrobinson.com

or use the code below on your phone

Contents

The Kissing Ball *1*

Love and The Royal Society *42*

The Widow and the Gentleman *86*

Sir Robert, the Dog and the Dimple *117*

Storming The Citadel *149*

An Excerpt from *Héloise Says No* *168*

The Kissing Ball

1

The Branson family always held a party at the beginning of the Christmas season, on the 6th of December, St. Nicholas' Day. Though some purists held that bringing greens into the house before Christmas Eve was unlucky, great branches of red-berried holly were placed in urns around the foyer, and it was the habit of the house to hang a ball of ribboned mistletoe above the center of the entrance to the drawing room. This evening was no exception. A large kissing ball hung there in all its glory.

In spite of its allure, the even quite recently married ladies sailed under it on the arms of their husbands without apparently giving it a thought, and the older married ones seemed so far from expecting any show of affection that being on the arm of their husband appeared contact enough. It was seldom indeed that it occurred to any of the gentlemen in either case to kiss their wives. There must be something about marriage, thought Quentin Stapleton as he watched the arrivals, that makes a man impervious to his wife's charms. Only two or three years before, he reflected, the younger men and women, then still sighing on the altar of unrequited love, had doubtless looked upon it as the occasion to steal a normally forbidden embrace. Now, all passion past, the kissing ball might as well be a cabbage.

But it was still always fun, he chuckled to himself, to see how the unwed maidens handled it. The more timid of them tended to scuttle to one side of the wide doorway, thus avoiding the perilous center and the chance that a waiting gentleman might take the opportunity to plant a kiss upon their cheek. Not that they would so dislike being kissed. Most of them had never felt the lips of any man but their father or possibly other older male family member, and the thought of the warm imprint of those belonging to a younger member of the opposite sex did indeed cause a flutter in their chaste bosoms. But they were so afraid the matrons clustered around the edges of the large room watching the comings and goings with eagle eyes would stigmatize them as *fast,* that they dared not appear to court such an eventuality.

The bolder young ladies walked quite slowly straight through the middle of the doorway and might possibly even slow their steps just a little when the crucial moment was reached. Not to encourage any available gentleman, you understand, but merely to show they didn't give a fig for the old-fashioned notions of the tabbies observing them narrowly through their lorgnettes. If a young man did take the opportunity to snatch a kiss, well, it always came as *such* a shock that the young lady in question would utter a shriek and tap the kisser sharply on the chest with her fan, before opening it and fanning herself as if she were on the brink of a faint.

What none of the beauties did was to walk slowly into the center of the doorway, right under the green and white ball with its red ribbons, and stand there, immobile, scanning the room, while her pink cheek, framed by a mass of copper curls held back by a diamond clip, presented itself deliciously to any comer. But this one did. Quentin Stapleton was certain he had never seen her before in his life. He would have remembered. She was rather above average height with a delicious figure over which her golden gown shimmered as if over the top of a very firm jelly. The lure was irresistible. He took three long strides and was by her side and placing his lips on the aforementioned cheek, so wonderfully soft and cool, before either she or anyone else could move.

She was certainly startled, but instead of striking him with her fan, she placed one shapely white hand on the lapel of his superfine long-tailed coat and looked up at him, her dark brown eyes wide. She saw a pair of bright blue eyes under a shock of almost black hair and a teasing smile. His black coat lay without a wrinkle over broad shoulders. He turned his gaze up to the ball of mistletoe then down again into her eyes. She saw the direction of his glance and looked up there herself.

"Oh!" she said in a pleasant voice, "how silly of me. I didn't see it. I was looking for someone."

"Then it's my immeasurably good fortune you should have chosen just that spot to stop and look," replied Quentin. "I count it as a Christmas blessing."

She laughed unaffectedly. "What an elegant thing to say, Mr....?"

"Stapleton. Quentin Stapleton. At your service, Ma'am." He bowed.

"Well, Mr. Stapleton, I'm Laura Wentworth. I'm pleased to make your acquaintance." She stepped back and executed a rather cursory curtsey.

"Whom were you looking for?" he asked. "I must say, I hope he or she is not here, so you will talk to me." He drew her into the room.

"My fiancé," she said. "I was expecting to meet him here. No doubt I should have waited for the butler to present me to the hosts, but he was momentarily occupied and I just wandered in."

Quentin Stapleton's heart, usually a most reliable of organs and not given to somersaults or leaps, fell to his brilliantly shiny shoes.

"Your fiancé?" he repeated dumbly, "Who is he?"

"Nicholas Branson. This is where he lives, isn't it?"

"Nicky Branson is your fiancé?" he said, unable to conceal his surprise.

"Yes. Why are you looking like that?"

"Oh, er... No reason. I'm just a little surprised. I... er know Nicky well and he... well, he never mentioned being betrothed to... er, you."

"Well, he may have forgotten. It was all arranged so very long ago, you see, and I think our letter informing him of our coming may not have arrived. We heard nothing in return, but the post is very unreliable. And then Mama has been unwell, and couldn't come this evening. She's finding the cold weather quite a trial. She's completely unused to it, of course, and has had a dreadful grippe."

"Miss Wentworth, I know I must seem amazingly obtuse. Do I understand that Nicky may have forgotten he was betrothed to you and the letter reminding him may not have arrived? Arrived from where?"

"From India. Oh dear, I know it must seem a strange story."

"Why don't you sit down and tell me about it," said Quentin, leading her to a small sofa set against the wall. "First I'll send one of the footmen to look for Nicky. He's probably... er, in the billiard room."

In fact, he rather thought he was with his lady love, but he didn't say so.

He left her for a moment to tell the butler to find the son of the house and when he did, to make him wait in the library and come and tell him.

"This is not a joke, Grimshaw," said Quentin seriously. "I need to see him before he goes back into the drawing room. It's important. And if Miss Thomas is with him, get rid of her somehow."

2

When Quentin Stapleton came back into the drawing room he saw that his old friend Ferdy Wilson had already spotted the newcomer and was perched on the sofa next to her.

"Make like a hoop and roll away, old boy," he said, coming up to them. "Miss Wentworth is… er, an old friend. We have a lot to catch up on."

"Known you m'whole life, Quen," responded Ferdy with surprise. "And I've never met Miss Wentworth before."

"As I said, we've catching up to do. Push off, old chap!"

Ferdy raised his eyebrows in disbelief, but bowed and left. Quentin took two glasses of champagne from a passing footman's tray, and sat down next to Miss Wentworth, handing her one.

"Now, Miss Wentworth, tell me the whole story," he said with the smile that had made him a favorite with the ladies for the last six seasons.

She took a sip of the champagne. "My father was best friends with Nicholas's father before going to India to make his fortune. When we were born, Nicholas in London and then I in India, our fathers pledged us to each other. They corresponded infrequently over the years, but when they did, they looked forward to the future joining of our families. My father spoke of it many times, and I have Mr. Branson's letters replying in the same vein. My father died four months ago after quite a long illness. My mother wrote to inform his old friend, and to say we were returning to England. It was my father's dying wish that we do so and that I be married to the son of his old friend. But it was all such a rush. We wanted to leave before the monsoons set in, so we packed up and were on the boat before you could say knife. I've been in London a few weeks but I haven't been anywhere. I needed to have some gowns made. The ones brought from India that I thought were so nice, I realized were dreadfully outdated. I kept expecting to hear from Nicholas, but when I didn't, I realized our letters must not have arrived. I saw the announcement of this party in the newspaper and came. I know it's not quite the thing, but I felt sure when Mrs. Branson knew who I was, she would introduce me."

"I'm afraid Mrs. Branson died last year."

"Oh dear! I'm so sorry. I don't believe my father knew. I'm sure he would have said something, though he was ill for quite a long time and not really capable of keeping up with things."

"Mr. Branson Senior was very cut up over it. I shouldn't be surprised if he never wrote. He came in earlier this evening to welcome the guests. But he seemed overcome, and disappeared. According to Nicky, he only held the party to honor the memory of his wife, who insisted on holding a party on the 6th of December every year. Nicholas is both her husband's and her son's name, you see."

Quentin stopped and thought for a moment before saying with some hesitation, "Forgive me for presuming to ask you questions that only a genuinely long-time friend could ask, but it didn't concern you that you might take Nicky in dislike? Or he you? Though," he added with a disarming smile, "that would hardly seem possible."

She smiled back. "You do say the most charming things! You must be one of the men my old governess used to warn me about. She used to tell me, *the more charming the words, the colder the heart.* But I think she had been jilted in her youth and had a very poor opinion of smooth-talking men ever after."

Quentin wondered if Miss Wentworth's governess had been right. He knew that until just a few minutes ago his heart had never been touched, though he was famous for his charm.

But Miss Wentworth was continuing. "But to answer your question, I thought that we would like each other sufficiently for marriage. I assumed Mr. Branson would have... other interests, and I might, too. Isn't that how it works? In India the English married couples I knew were usually like that. Many of them had hardly met before being wed, so they weren't in love. But it seemed to work well enough. There was even sometimes a degree of affection."

It was true that the older married couples of Quentin's experience had been married for convenience' sake rather than love, and often led very separate lives. He had himself been the beneficiary of the company of wives with little affection for their husbands. Thinking about it now, he realized that he would never be prepared to accept such a situation for himself. Anyway, these days love matches were becoming much more common. But he was saved from having to comment by the arrival of the butler, who announced in a low voice that Mr. Branson was in the library awaiting his pleasure.

In fact, Nicky Branson's exact words had been, "What the devil does Quen want? Tell him I'm busy. I'll give him five minutes."

Quentin gave Miss Wentworth his arm and led her to the library. When he opened the door and shepherded her in, the scion of the family was in front of the fire, his rather short legs spread in front of him, a sullen look on his face that was at odds with his rather weak chin. He had what looked like a large brandy in his hand. When he saw Miss Wentworth, he partially straightened himself and made as if to stand up, but the expression on his face remained.

"Who're you?" he asked gracelessly.

"Miss Wentworth, this is Nicholas Branson. Nicky, this is Miss Wentworth," said Quentin quickly, "your... er, fiancée."

"My what?" Nicholas bolted up and goggled at them both.

"From India," explained his friend.

Nicholas stared at them. Then a look of realization came over his face. "You don't mean you're the daughter of the chap m' father's been talking about on and off all these years?"

"Yes," said Miss Wentworth. "I'm sorry to say, my father died earlier this year. They were the greatest of friends. We were promised to each other." And seeing his look of disbelief, she added, "Didn't you know?"

"No I did not! My God, it can't be true!"

"I'm afraid it is. I have your father's letters. And almost the last thing my father said was I was to come to London and find you."

Nicholas drank a hefty slug from the glass that was still in his hand. "My God," he said again. "My God!" He slumped back into the chair.

"Mr. Branson, Nicholas," said Laura Wentworth, "I take it your father told you nothing of the letter we sent before leaving India?"

"What letter? No, he's said nothing about any letter." A look of comprehension came into his face. "No wonder he blew up just now when I told him I was thinking of popping the question to Amy." Mr. Branson looked like a man passing his whole life in review. "He mentioned a few times over the years that his old friend had a daughter, and always looked like he was going to say more, but Mama always shushed him. She was a fine woman, my Mama. She never would have thought me bound to a woman I'd never met, living on the other side of the world. But since she died he's been all to pieces. Told me he would never agree to Amy and he'd cut me off without a bean if I married to displease him!"

There was a silence. Then Miss Wentworth took a deep breath and said, "I understand then, Mr. Branson, that you wish to offer marriage to Miss… Amy, and your father is refusing to allow you because of his promise to my father?"

"That seems to be about the sum of it," mumbled Nicholas.

"And you desire to marry the lady because you love her?"

"Yes, of course, what else? I ain't a fortune hunter. Got enough blunt of my own. Well, I will have if I ain't cut off."

"And I suppose a marriage of convenience is out of the question?"

"Good God, of course it is! In any case, I know Amy wouldn't countenance being the Other Woman."

"No, I can quite see she wouldn't," said Miss Wentworth, sadly.

There seemed little to say after that. Laura drew herself up and wished both gentlemen good night. She made as if to leave the library, but Quentin took her arm.

"Come, Miss Wentworth," he said. "Allow me to take you home. My carriage is outside."

"There's no need, I can have the butler call a hackney. My maid is waiting in the hall."

"There's room for the three of us in my carriage. 'Night, Nicky. Good luck!"

Quentin firmly placed Miss Wentworth's arm under his and led her out into the hall.

3

Nicholas Branson heaved himself out of the armchair and walked irresolutely into the drawing room. He spotted Amy Thomas talking to one of the other young women, who was nodding with a look of condolence on her face. Nicky guessed Amy was pouring out her woes regarding her future with himself. He made his way over to her side and arrived in time to hear her saying,

"It's just too bad! Nicky and I can only think his father has lost his mind somehow. He was so downcast at the death of Nicky's Mama, he seems to have become another person. Oh, there you are, I was just telling Judith…."

"Yes, I know what you were telling her. I need to speak to you, Amy," and turning to the other damsel, "Judith, keep this under your hat, for heaven's sake!"

"Of course I will," replied that maiden earnestly, her rather plain round face suffused with a look of pity mixed with a violent desire to know what Nicky wanted to talk to Amy about. To her intense disappointment, he led his inamorata away.

"She won't, you know," he said as soon as he was out of earshot, "Dammed girl's a positive rattle."

"I know, but I was so unhappy! I had to tell someone! I was ready to drop when you told me your father absolutely forbids an engagement with me. I was already thinking of a spring wedding!"

He took her into the library and closed the door.

"We have to be quick," said Amy. "If Mama sees I'm gone again and guesses I'm with you, she'll think you're popping the question.

She's bound to ask me, and what am I to say?" Her rather protuberant blue eyes filled with tears.

"Look here, Amy, don't cry," said Nicky, beginning to wish he'd never heard the word *marriage* in his life. "I know why m'father went into a fit when I suggested a betrothal with you. He had a very good friend from his Cambridge days who went to India. Evidently, his pockets were to let and he had no expectations over here. Married a good sort of woman by all accounts and off he went. But he kept in touch with the old man. Well, I knew they had a girl, but what I didn't know is they pledged we'd be married one day. He never told me about it, I'm pretty sure, because Mama wouldn't let him. But now she's gone, and he's all at sea, he's damned well clutching onto the old plan."

"But where is this girl?" cried Amy wildly. "Is she here?"

"Not any more. I told her I wanted to marry you and she pushed off with old Quentin."

"Does she want to marry you?"

"Apparently. She's come all this way to do it. Her Pa's dead, and on his deathbed told her to seek me out."

"What's she like?" Amy's feminine curiosity overcame the more important questions of the moment. "Is she pretty?"

"I don't know. She's all right. Tall and well, you know," he made a vague shape with his hands.

"You mean she's, er, well built?"

"Something like that. Red hair."

"Red hair! Does she have freckles?" Miss Thomas was envisioning an unattractively large woman with frizzy red hair and freckles. She wasn't altogether displeased with the image. After all, even Nicky's father could see she was a much more attractive option. But her beloved let her down.

"Freckles? How should I know? Don't think so."

"Oh, I wish I'd seen her!"

"Good Lord, Amy! We've got more important things to think about."

"I know what to do!" said Amy, clapping her hands together. "I'll go and see her. I'll tell her she's ruining both our lives and she's bound to give you up. She doesn't love you! She doesn't even know you! Then she can explain to your father and he'll be released from any obligation!"

"D'you think so?" said Nicholas, doubtfully. "But what about what her Pa wanted when he was dying? Anyway, if she's come home without a sou, she might see me as a meal-ticket."

"Can't you pay her off?"

"Not at the moment, maybe later when my father curls up his toes."

"Oh," said Amy. "Don't you have any money? We're not going to be poor, are we? *My* Papa won't let me marry you if we are!"

"Of course not! I can support a wife, all right and tight. But I can't be giving Miss Wentworth money—why she could ask a king's ransom!"

"Yes, I suppose she could! You *are* a catch, Nicky!" said Miss Thomas, fondly.

Meanwhile, Quentin Stapleton had driven home the would-be fiancée. Any conversation was naturally hindered by the presence of her maid, but as he saw her to her door, he said that with her permission, he would wait on her the following afternoon. Then he bowed and was gone.

Miss Wentworth was staying in a rather unfashionable area of London. She entered the narrow hallway and went immediately up to see her mother. That lady was reposing on top of her bed, swathed in shawls and coverlets, in spite of the blazing fire in the hearth.

"Laura! Come in and close the door! The draft is dreadful! I can't believe I used to live in this terrible cold. I simply can't get warm!"

Mrs. Wentworth had been lovely in her youth, and she was still very pretty. She had a fine head of golden-white hair above a practically unlined forehead. In spite of being huddled in blankets she had a firm chin, cheeks that dimpled when she smiled and the wide, clear gaze Laura had inherited. Other than that, Laura was her father's daughter with his fine carriage and well-developed body.

"Tell me what happened. Did the Bransons greet you with open arms?" she asked. "I'm sorry I wasn't up to coming. My cold is nearly better, but I didn't want to chance it by going out in the damp."

"Quite the reverse, I'm sorry to say, Mama. Well, Mr. Branson wasn't there. Apparently he's still mourning the loss of his wife a year ago. His son Nicholas was there and not at all pleased to see me! He didn't know anything about the promise. His father hadn't mentioned we were coming and anyway he's in love with another woman! But his father won't hear of it. It seems he's attached to the idea of carrying out the promise to his old friend. What a tangle!"

"I remember Branson Senior. He was a nice fellow, but always the type to stick to a thing once he'd decided on it. But you must speak to him. You know as well as I that your Papa would never have held you to a promise that would make everyone unhappy. He was always only too flexible! I'd go with you, but with this cold…. The only thing is, my dear, I don't know how many months we can continue to live like this. You know your father left his affairs in a dreadful muddle. I loved him dearly, but he was never any good with money. And we simply had to buy ourselves some decent gowns to go about in, or we would certainly have been regarded as a couple of freaks. But I had no idea things were so expensive here! If you don't marry young Branson, I don't know what we shall do."

"I know, Mama, I know. I'll go to see his father. There must be a way of sorting this all out. Now you get into bed. I'll have Mary bring up another warm brick and some warm milk. By the way, God bless her! She sat in the hall at the Branson's pretending to be my personal maid, when all she is really is a sort of combined house and kitchen maid. I was so lucky she wasn't afraid to come and keep me countenance. Good night, Mama, dearest."

She kissed her mother lovingly on the cheek and went into her own room. Knowing the straitened circumstances of the household, she kept no fire in there as a rule, so the air was frigid. She quickly undressed, brushed her teeth, and leaped into bed. The brick placed there before she went out was almost cold by now, but a faint residue of the heat still remained. At least, the bed wasn't as cold as the rest of the room. Like her mother, she was finding the damp, chill climate of London in the winter hard to get used to. She had been born and raised in a climate where the heat had been a problem, not the cold. She remembered fondly the bungalow in the hills where they went in the hottest months. It overlooked a lake surrounded by flame trees and rhododendrons. She smiled as she thought about it, and soon fell asleep.

4

The next afternoon, Laura was not really surprised to receive a call from Nicholas Branson's Amy. That young lady came in, casting surreptitious glances around the rather shabby interior. Having greeted her, Laura commented upon her glances.

"Yes, it is a bit mean, isn't it? That's the problem with hiring a house without any knowledge of the place you're going to. Mama and I had no idea, but by the time we got here and sorted ourselves out, then Mama caught a dreadful cold, we haven't had a chance to do anything about it." *There*, she thought to herself, *that should dispel the notion that we're poor relations.*

In fact, Miss Thomas was confused. Her hostess's gown was of the first stare and obviously costly, but the house, well...

"Oh, I hadn't really noticed," she lied. "I hope you won't mind my visiting you like this, Miss Wentworth. I know we've not been formally introduced, but Nicholas told me all about you and I feel as if I know you."

This was very far from the truth. She knew nothing about her rival, and she could see immediately everything Nicky had said was wrong. He had called her red-haired. Red haired! She had the most glorious copper curls and was not remotely freckled! And yes, she was tall, much taller than Amy herself was, but she wasn't remotely fleshy. She was just... well, Miss Thomas was not at all fanciful, but she was forcibly reminded of the figure on the prow of a ship. And she was wearing a lovely green velvet day dress that accentuated the lights in her brown eyes. Amy had thought it would be so easy to talk to this pretender to the hand of her Nicky, but now she found herself strangely tongue-tied.

Laura came to her aid. "I expect you want to talk to me about this tangle. Mr. Branson wants to marry you, but his Papa wants him to marry me."

Put like that, it sounded so simple. Amy leaped at it. "Oh yes, Miss Wentworth! That's it exactly! Would you talk to Nicky's father and tell him you don't want to marry his son? I mean, you can't be in love with him. You don't even know him! Whereas I...," her voice tailed off.

"Well, I certainly don't want to be the cause of your, or his, unhappiness. But I should tell you my father died thinking I'd come to London and marry his friend's son. Of course, neither Papa nor I had any idea his son's heart was given to another. It would be on my conscience if I didn't talk it over with Mr. Branson. So I shall do that."

"Oh, thank you, thank you!" Amy thought for a moment. "Would you be so kind as to write him a note now? I could carry it to Nicky's and he'll give it to his father."

Miss Wentworth complied. Going to the standish, she wrote a brief note requesting an interview with her father's old friend. She sealed it and gave it to Miss Thomas. The two women seemed to have nothing to talk about after that, for Amy had no interest in anything outside her immediate experience, and Laura knew nothing of her visitor's life. In a very short time the young woman was taking her leave and the hostess was breathing a sigh of relief.

Not thirty minutes later, the knocker sounded again and Quentin Stapleton was shown in. He paid no attention at all to his surroundings, but came straight to Miss Wentworth and bowed over her hand.

"I was afraid you would be downcast by the events yesterday evening," he said with a smile, once she had invited him to sit down. "But I see the opposite is true. No one could look less downcast. You are in full bloom."

Laura thought the same might be said of him. He was wearing a dark grey coat over fawn-colored pantaloons that disappeared into a pair of highly polished boots. A houndstooth check waistcoat lay over spotless linen and around his neck was a shining white cloth in complicated folds.

"I repeat what I said last night, Mr. Stapleton," she said with a laugh. "You are just the sort of man my governess warned me about. But I thank you for the pretty compliment. I don't know about full bloom. Both my mother and I are having an awful time with the cold and damp. I feel it more likely the flower may wither on the stalk."

"Then it's obvious you must come to a ball tonight at Lady March's. It will get so insufferably hot we Londoners won't be able to stand it. But it will suit you perfectly. Say you will come!"

"But will the hostess not object to an unknown woman being thrust upon her?"

"No, I shall send a note saying I'll be bringing a young lady newly arrived in town from overseas whom I have persuaded that an introduction to the *ton* at my Lady March's Christmas Ball is all one needs to be accepted anywhere. I have no doubt she'll be delighted."

Laura laughed unaffectedly. "You really are dreadful! Do you always get what you want?"

Since Quentin Stapleton did in fact usually get exactly what he wanted, he could only answer with a shrug.

This time was no exception. At nine o'clock that evening the knocker sounded and he was there to help her into his carriage.

The night before she had been in a daze, and the carriage had been out of the light from the flambeaux in front of the Bransons' house, so that she had not noticed the Coat of Arms on the door. Tonight she saw it clearly enough: a black lion rampant on a white field, held aloft on either side by two more lions, white this time and with long curly tongues. The motto was written beneath, but it was too small to read at that time of night. She commented upon it as soon as they were both settled.

"Yes, my grandfather insisted on having the Arms on all the family conveyances and I suppose we've never done anything about it. I don't even notice it myself."

"But have you a noble family?"

"Well, yes, I suppose so. I'm only a Viscount, though. Nothing grand. A very low-level Viscount, I assure you. I usually don't mention it. It raises people's expectations."

From this, Laura understood her friend was the scion of an impoverished noble family. She made light of it. "It sounds grand to me. Should I curtsey when I enter your presence?"

"No. I'd prefer you stand stock still under a ball of mistletoe so I could kiss you again."

"Oh yes, I'd forgotten that," said Laura with a laugh. "What with all the other revelations, it went right out of my mind. That was very bad of you, you know, now that I think about it. It's a good thing I'm not a vaporish kind of Miss. I might have had a spasm!"

Quentin was not used to having his kisses forgotten so easily, but answered lightly, "You didn't look at all vaporish. If you had, I shouldn't have wanted to kiss you."

"No," agreed his companion. "I'm too big for that. I've never been able to pretend to be weak. Do you know, I've never fainted in my life!"

"Neither have I," said her partner. "So that's something we don't have to worry about!"

By now they had arrived at their destination. The carriage drew up in front of a large Mayfair house, illuminated by huge flaming torches in iron holders on either side of the front door. A carpet led up the wide steps to the door, which was open, giving a view of a large hall brightly lit by branched crystal chandeliers. Carriages were milling thickly around the entrance and ladies and gentlemen were picking their way through them to the front steps. Quentin placed his lady's hand firmly under his arm and led her through the throng, nodding here and there to acquaintances, and managing to make swift progress in spite of the people in their path. In no time, it seemed, they were in the front hall, their cloaks were taken, Lord Stapleton's tall curly-brimmed beaver was removed, and they were waiting to be announced at the ballroom door.

The immense room was heated by four fireplaces, two on each side, together with innumerable candles blazing from chandeliers down the length of the room. In the corners enormous branches of holly were standing in waist-high urns, but, as far as Laura could discern, there were no kissing balls. Against one wall in the center of the room there was a raised platform on which a number of musicians were disposed, some tuning their instruments, some just looking at the crowd.

It was, as Quentin had foretold, very warm, for which Laura could only be very grateful. She was wearing her one ballgown. It was of a heavy silk in a dull ruby red, the bodice embroidered with pearls, low cut with short sleeves. The train could be caught up on the wrist for dancing. She wore long gloves the same color as her dress, and on her right wrist a bracelet shone with diamonds. She wore nothing around her neck, but from her ears hung a pair of diamond drop earrings. They were amongst the very few pieces of jewelry she owned and matched the bracelet and the diamond clip she again wore in her abundant copper curls. The set had belonged to her maternal grandmother whom she had never known but who had been, her mother said, a woman of limited means but excellent taste. She had preferred to wear no jewelry at all than to wear something second rate.

Laura had been wearing her cloak when Quentin had picked her up, and when he saw her now, as it were, revealed, he caught his breath. She looked glorious. The pearls on her bodice highlighted her magnificent bosom and the diamonds shone in the candle and firelight.

Lady March and her husband turned out to be a couple nearer her mother's age than Laura's own. They greeted her kindly and asked where she had just come from. When she said India, Lord March said immediately, "Then we must have the Plimptons invite you to their Christmas dinner next week. Old Plimpton spent years over there. He'll want to hear what's been going on since he left."

"I remember them!" said Laura with pleasure. "Of course, I was much younger then, so I didn't exactly socialize with them, but my mother will be delighted to see them again."

"Then I'll make sure you both receive an invitation," said Lord March. "I suppose you'll be there, Stapleton?"

"Of course. Wouldn't miss it," said Quentin. "One of the highlights of the season. Not as unmissable as this ball, of course, Lady March. Christmas wouldn't be Christmas without it." He smiled down at her.

Lady March shook her head and tapped him with her fan. "I'm far too old to be gulled by a man like you, no matter how good his address," she said. Then turned to Laura. "Don't let him take you in, my dear," she said. "He's a rogue."

"I had already realized that," said Laura. "But I think I'm up to his tricks." She smiled at him.

Quentin's usually placid heart performed the same somersault it had the day before, but he said lightly as they walked into the room, "I didn't ask, but do you, in fact, care to dance?"

He had sudden misgivings that they might not be up-to-date in that respect in India, but his partner answered gaily, "Oh yes! I love to dance. Of course, in India we only did country and Scottish dances. It was when we were on the boat coming over that I first heard about the Cotillion and the Waltz. Luckily, one of the ship's officers was assigned to bring us all up to snuff. We had lessons and two balls while we were at sea. Mama was not at all happy to see a young man's arm around my waist at first. She wondered what Mr. Branson would say if he saw it. Now we know we need not have worried. He would have told me to carry on and good luck!"

"We will get dance cards from the ball master, and I shall sign my name to the waltzes. I feel it my duty to save you from the rakes and rattles here tonight."

"You mean the *other* rakes and rattles!" laughed Laura, but willingly allowed him to sign his name to two waltzes.

Quentin Stapleton, of course, knew everyone at the ball, and introduced her all around. As a result, her dance card was filled in moments. She scarcely had time to exchange a few words with him the rest of the evening, except during the waltzes. Then, the feel of his strong warm hand in the small of her back sent an altogether unaccustomed shiver through her body.

"Are you cold?" he asked, solicitously. "Shall I fetch your shawl?

"Oh, no," she said, "in fact, I think I'm warm for the first time since I arrived. I don't know what made me shiver."

But she did.

5

The following day, Laura received a note from Mr. Branson Senior saying he would be delighted to see her any time that afternoon, so three o'clock saw her being ushered into his study. It was a room full of rather dusty old books that looked as if they hadn't been moved in years, and smelled not unpleasantly of cigar smoke. Her host rose and pressed her hand meaningfully, then bade her sit down. He was a man of medium height, stocky like his son, and with what she saw was a weak chin hidden under a well-groomed beard.

She sniffed the scent of cigars appreciatively. "The scent of cigars will always make me think of my father," she said.

"Ah, yes, many's the time we smoked together in the old days," said Mr. Branson, "smoked and talked... and lived! What times we had! He was everything I was not: lively, popular, full of adventure. I was always more quiet and given to reflection, but how he drew me out! When I would hesitate to go to parties, he would drag me into the thick of them. Where I was likely to spend an afternoon reading, he would pull me onto the river—the Cam, you know—and never mind if he upset the boat, trying to pick a water lily for his latest love! Everywhere he went, there was fun! Those were some of the best days of my life. When he said he was going to seek his fortune in India, I was devastated. I tried to persuade him to stay, but he said there was no future for a man like him here in England. And he was fortunate enough to find a wife who would follow him. A courageous woman, your mother. Tell me, how is she?"

Laura had been reflecting that what Mr. Branson said was true. Her father had been a devil-may-care kind of fellow, full of spirit and new ideas. But what had no doubt made a marvelous companion for youth, made a less than successful husband and father later on. Now she replied, "My mother is feeling the cold dreadfully and is recovering from a nasty grippe. I'm sure that as soon as she's well enough, she'll be delighted to see you again."

"Poor woman! She must be feeling her loss most deeply, too."

"Yes, of course." Laura did not elaborate. In fact, though her mother had loved her husband, as the years went by, his rather profligate spending combined with an inability to stick very long to any gainful occupation had made their lives difficult. There was no denying that it was because of him that, in the end, they had left India with rather little.

Mr. Branson seemed to read her mind. "You will forgive my asking, Miss Wentworth, but I feel my lifelong friendship with your father permits me to ask an indiscreet question. Did my old friend make the fortune he sought by going so far away?"

Laura decided there was no need to wash all their linen in public. "Well, I daresay he did not do as well as he had hoped, but I don't think he ever regretted his decision to leave England."

But her host was more astute than she had realized. "Ah, you are protective of your father, as a daughter should be. I commend you for it. But I often wondered, from reading his letters, how he was getting along. He would talk of plans, and the next time I heard, it would be something completely different. I must say, it caused me some disquiet." He said nothing for a moment, his eyes fixed on a past only he could see. Then, "But you will have no need to worry. When you are married to my son, you will have enough and more to provide the elegancies of life. And your dear mother will not be forgotten."

For a moment Laura almost thought, *why not*? Here was the solution to their problems. She could keep her promise to her father and provide for her mother in one swoop. But her good sense quickly intervened.

"But, my dear sir, surely you are not still envisioning a match between Nicholas and myself? You know he's in love with Miss Thomas, and she with him. It would be cruelty to force him into marriage with me."

"Nonsense! He knows his duty. It is to wed where I direct. There's no question of Miss Thomas. It's a passing fancy, nothing more."

"But, sir, I don't think I could be happy coming between two people who love each other! I know my father would not expect me to keep a promise to him under these conditions."

"Ah! You promised him! Then it must and shall be so! Remembering your duty to him will bring you all the happiness you need. As soon as your mother is well enough, we will plan your nuptials."

Laura realized she had made a mistake in mentioning the word *promise*. "But sir, you must have known couples who were forced into a marriage of convenience and who have been dreadfully unhappy as a consequence."

"I know it is the modern idea that a couple should meet and *fall in love*, as the saying is, but that is just a new-fangled notion. What was good enough for me and for my father, and even, I'm sure, for his father before him, is good enough for Nicholas. Why, I had barely seen my dear wife Hermione before we were betrothed, and yet we were very happy together."

Laura thought that was probably because Nicky's father was a man easily led. That weak chin told the tale. He had been drawn to her father because he was an up-and-at-'em kind of person. She didn't doubt that the late Mrs. Branson was cut from the same cloth. But she realized it was useless to argue. Like many weak persons, he was obviously stubborn.

Not wanting to appear intractable, she accepted his offer of a glass of Madeira and stayed another half hour, chatting about life in India and more particularly, her father's adventures, which she cast in the best possible light. When they finally parted, it was on cordial terms, with her promising to return the following week for more discussions of her father, which, it seemed, along with contemplating the past with his dear wife, were Mr. Branson's sole delights.

As she went home, Laura reflected how much her ideas had changed in the last three days. She had been happy to follow her father's wishes and had been fully prepared to marry a man she didn't know, to bear his children and make an agreeable home for him. She thought she would probably grow to hold him in some affection and having a home and family would fulfil her. But a tall man with laughing blue eyes and a strong, warm hand in the small of her back had shown her that feelings towards a man could be much more than mere affection. Marrying for comfort and stability no longer seemed enough. But there still remained the twin problems of Mr. Branson's stubborn adherence to an idea formed twenty years ago, and the fact that she and her mother simply could not carry on much longer without funds. What was she to do?

6

Were it not for the nagging worry about her and her mother's future, Laura would have very much enjoyed the Christmas season in London. She had, of course, never seen the holiday celebrated in England. In India the British contingent had naturally kept the traditions alive. There were parties and dinners featuring foods as close to the Christmas goose and plum pudding as could be contrived. Just as back home in England, presents were exchanged on Christmas Eve. Christmas Day was always a quiet family time after church in the morning. Here in London, though, the very air smelled of Christmas. It was full of the delicious scent of the street vendors' roasted chestnuts and the greens brought up from the country: bunches of ivy, holly, and mistletoe. Others sold dried fruits and sweet meats and little fancies tied up in colored paper. Added to this throng were the carolers who would set up on street corners, a cap on the ground for the pennies of the passers-by. *God Rest Ye Merry Gentlemen* and *Good Christian Men, Rejoice* rang out over the top of the clatter of horse's hooves, the cries of sweeps, linkboys and pie-sellers. She found it thrilling.

When Quentin found out she was taking a hackney just for the pleasure of riding through the streets, he began stopping by on the pretext of bringing a posy of flowers, a packet of tea or a pastry from Gunther's for her mother. It wasn't long before he became a favorite and trusted visitor, so that when he suggested a turn in his carriage, Mrs. Wentworth encouraged her daughter to go. There would always be a hot brick for her feet and a heavy horsehair blanket for her lap. She would sit back against the cushioned squabs and laugh with her escort over the curious sights and sounds that met their eyes. One afternoon he took her as far as the Vauxhall Gardens. The perfumed shrubs were bare, and the trees leafless, but the lanterns still glowed as the sun went down and a few hardy performers performed cartwheels and juggling tricks for the visitors. Walking next to Quentin, Laura felt at ease and above all, safe.

This was an aspect of the male-female relationship that had not occurred to her. Her father had never been a very safe sort of person. In fact, as she got older, Laura had found herself trying to protect her Mama from the inevitable disappointment of his latest venture. She had somehow thought that in marriage she would carry on looking after herself and her mother, and then her children. But being with a man who foresaw problems and took steps to prevent them was a new experience for her. Quentin brought an umbrella if it looked like rain; he bespoke refreshment before they got where they were going; once, when he saw that an approaching carriage was going to splash her, he stood in front and took the full brunt of the muddy water on his many-caped cloak. He then laughed it off and refused to shorten their walk to go home and change.

When she expressed a wish to hear *The Messiah* at the Theatre Royal in Covent Garden, Quentin somehow acquired tickets, though it had been listed as sold out. Apparently there had been some disapproval years before when the religious oratorio was first performed in this secular setting, but now it was extremely popular. Laura had actually sung in a very abbreviated performance of it one Christmas when the music director of the Anglican church had been both capable of producing a simplified version and conducting the small church choir. Unfortunately, he had moved on and the performance had never been repeated. Now, the glorious sound sung by a full choir filled her heart and made her clutch her escort's arm. He smiled down at her rapt expression and his heart filled too, though not with the music. At the end of the Hallelujah Chorus, she turned her swimming eyes to his and met in them such a look that it took her breath clean away. In the carriage home they were both unusually silent.

The next day, though she would have liked nothing more than to stay at home and think, she felt compelled to keep her word to Mr. Branson and go to see him again. She spent an hour or so with the older man, Mary waiting in the hall as before, listening to the wonderful adventures he had had with her father and, when she felt compelled to add something, adding stories of her own.

Finally, he said, "My dear! I so look forward to the time when you will be in the house all the time and we may have such conversations whenever we want. How goes your mother? It wants only her full recovery for us to plan your nuptials."

Her heart full of dread, Laura replied, "I'm afraid that though she is gradually improving, she is still quite poorly. I fear we must wait until the New Year. We cannot do anything before then."

Just let me keep delaying the evil moment, she thought to herself. *Surely something will happen!*

"Of course, my dear. I would not desire anything that would set her back. I have fine memories of her, too. A beautiful, courageous woman. The perfect spouse for my dear old friend, I always thought."

Laura smilingly agreed, and shortly after took her leave. The butler was showing her to the door, when Nicholas surged from the library and urgently took her arm.

"I wish to talk to Miss Wentworth, Grimshaw. I'll see her out afterwards."

No sooner was the library door closed than Mr. Branson Junior spoke. "Miss Wentworth! The most disastrous thing has happened. Amy has broken with me! She has written me a note. Look!"

Laura took the note thrust into her hands and read:

Dear Mr. Branson,

I'm sorry to inform you the understanding between us must now be at an end. My eyes have been opened to the kind of man you are.

You have made no attempt to convince your Father of your determination to marry me. It has been two weeks and you have done nothing. I can only assume you find the prospect of marriage to Miss Wentworth preferable.

Even if you do still have feelings for me, I need not say that I find a man unable to fight for the woman he says he loves unacceptable as a husband.

You never gave me a ring (indeed, I should have taken that as a sign!), so I have none to return.

With best wishes for your future happiness, I am,

Yours sincerely,
Amy Thomas

"What do you think of that, Miss Wentworth? How the devil did she think I could persuade my father? You know what he's like. He won't listen to reason! And what does she mean by *fight for the woman he says he loves*? Does she seriously think I could fight my own father?"

In fact, Miss Wentworth thought much the same as Amy. Had Nicholas actually done anything to persuade his father? Looking at his weak chin, she thought probably not. But at all costs, she had to keep Nicholas from telling him what Amy had said! That would be the end of it. She could just imagine Mr. Branson convincing his weak-willed son that Amy's dropping him proved what he had said all along, that their so-called love was just childish nonsense.

"I'm sure she doesn't mean it, Mr. Branson," she said soothingly. "Miss Thomas is very upset and not herself. I think you should write and reassure her of your undying love. That's what she wants, you know."

"D'you really think so?"

"Certainly. It's what I would want, in her place."

In fact, protestations of undying affection not followed up by action would be the last thing she would want, but she thought she understood Miss Thomas better than he did.

Her words seemed to convince Nicholas. "Then that's what I'll do. I say, thank you, Miss Wentworth. Mighty good of you. Puts you in a difficult spot, though. You wanted me yourself, I know, but we wouldn't suit, you see."

"Oh yes, I do see. You're quite right. We shouldn't suit at all."

7

For the few days after the *Messiah* evening, by what seemed like mutual though unspoken consent, Quentin and Laura saw nothing of each other. She lived in daily dread that word would come from Nicholas that all was indeed over between him and Amy, and his father was pushing for a wedding date. But she heard nothing from him either.

Then came the day of the Plimptons' Christmas dinner, always held the day before Christmas Eve. Lord and Lady March had been as good as their word and both ladies were invited. Contrary to what Laura had told Mr. Branson, her mother was doing much better. In fact, she had decided she was well enough to go out, and was looking forward to her first social invitation in London. Knowing they were almost certainly planning on taking a hackney, Quentin sent a note to say he would pick them up in his carriage. He was particularly solicitous of Mrs. Wentworth, himself placing the brick under her feet and making sure she was so wrapped in blankets that only the tip of her nose was visible. On the way to the Plimptons, Mrs. Wentworth chatted merrily about her first outing, but the other two passengers exchanged the merest pleasantries.

In spite of her worries, Laura quite enjoyed the dinner, though her palate, accustomed to accompaniments that were usually quite spiced, found the side dishes somewhat bland. There was goose and venison, vegetables like turnips in cream that she had never eaten before, carrots with raisins, stewed apples and at the end, a magnificent plum pudding was brought ablaze to the table to join the other sweets.

She sat close to her hostess while her mother was near the host at the other end of the table. Quentin was somewhere in the middle, royally entertaining the ladies on either side of him, to judge from the manipulation of fans, either to tap him on the arm or cover blushing giggles. Mrs. Plimpton plied her with questions about this person or that, most of whom were from an older generation and not her personal friends. But she was able to supply information about which of their children had married, and to whom, and how many grandchildren they had. This all interested her hostess mightily, and she was heard to declare afterwards that the Wentworth girl was quite charming. Her mother was found equally delightful by Mr. Plimpton, as she could bring him more accurate news of former acquaintances, especially those who were no longer so robust in their old age. This seemed to entertain her host, a hearty, red-faced individual who seemed pleased to hear of the misfortunes of former friends.

While the men were enjoying their port after dinner, the ladies retired to the drawing room, where an enormous log with other, smaller pieces piled on top, burned in the fireplace.

"Yes," said Mrs. Plimpton, when Laura remarked upon it. "The Yule log. We have one brought up from the country every year and try to keep it going until Twelfth Night. But we like to keep a piece to start the fire for the Christmas season next year, so we usually end up pulling it out before then. My dear! The complete tradition is only really possible in those baronial halls with fireplaces a man can stand up and turn around in. What we have here is positively mean!"

Since the fireplace in question was a lovely Adams piece, and Laura was comparing it to the very poor equivalent in their rented home, she gave no reply, but simply nodded.

As they drove home, Mrs. Wentworth was full of the delightful evening she had spent. She tried to get Laura to join in reviewing the delicacies they had eaten, what she had talked about with their hostess, and the beauty of the Plimptons' home. But Laura answered mechanically. The evening had brought home to her several things all at once.

First, for her mother to enjoy the sort of company and society she was born to, they would need a great deal more money. As it was, they could barely afford to stay in the second-rate establishment they presently occupied. It was in some ways fortunate Mama had been laid up for the first month of their stay in London, for she had not been exposed to the shortcomings of their position. How could they invite any of those ladies to tea, even, let alone host dinner parties? How long was it before their situation became widely known?

But worse than that, she had finally acknowledged to herself she was in love, and she was almost sure her feelings were reciprocated. She had found her eyes drawn irresistibly to Quentin Stapleton as he sat with the other ladies. She knew he had looked towards her, too, and once, their eyes had met. He had smiled at her and that shiver had gone down her spine. When the men joined the ladies in the drawing room, he had not gone straight to her. He had sat next to a number of the other guests and chatted cheerfully before finally joining her. Then his conversation had been light and inconsequential. She knew he was protecting her from gossip, for the fact they had been seen together on other occasions and had arrived together this evening had not passed unremarked. But it was impossible! It was a dreadful thing to admit, but she needed to marry where there was money. And what was it Quentin had said? He was *A very low-level Viscount.*

But as he had handed her into the carriage, he had pressed her hand and murmured, "I must talk to you. When may I find you alone?" As her mother was now up and about, she was usually in the drawing room and, apart from the dining room, the house had no other space for private conversation. Laura had shaken her head and muttered something in refusal, not knowing what she said. She knew what he wanted to ask her, and she knew she would have to refuse. She just couldn't bear it. As they neared their home, tears came uncontrollably to her eyes, so when he helped her down from the carriage, she kept her head lowered and would not look at him.

Hardly was she on the flag-way before she rushed indoors, muttering something disjointed to him and her mother, and fled to her bedchamber.

Mrs. Wentworth was astonished at her daughter's lack of manners. "I'm so sorry, Lord Stapleton," she said. "I hope Laura isn't coming down with what I have just recovered from. This behavior is so unlike her. I can't understand it."

But Quentin thought he understood, and made a polite but inconsequential response.

When her mother came into her room, Laura was face-down on her bed, sobbing as if her heart would break.

"Whatever is the matter, my dear?" she cried. "Have you the head-ache? Let me go and find my lavender water. That will help."

"No, no, Mama…," sobbed Laura. "It's not that!"

And out it all came: Miss Thomas had dropped Mr. Branson, and if his father learned of it, he would push all the harder for Laura to marry his son. But she didn't want to marry him! She was in love with Lord Stapleton! And she thought Lord Stapleton loved her! But how could she go back on her promise to her father if the man he had wanted her to marry was free and available because his would-be fiancée had left him, and it was all her fault? And poor Mr. Branson, he was already miserable because his wife had died, what would he do if his long-held desire concerning her marrying his son was also thwarted? And if she didn't marry Nicholas how would they live? He was well off. Lord Stapleton had told her he didn't have any money. Her words tumbled together; she was barely coherent. Her mother gently soothed her, until her passion had cried itself out.

Then she said, "Laura, my love, how can you think for a minute that there is any consideration more important than your happiness? Your father, for all his faults, would never have wanted you to keep your word to him if it meant your being unhappy. And what the two Mr. Bransons may do is their affair, not yours! You are in no way responsible for them! If Lord Stapleton wants to marry you and you want to marry him, there is no more to be said! We shall manage. We always have, and we always will. Now, I will ask Mary to bring you a glass of hot milk and another hot brick, and you will go to bed. You are exhausted by all this worrying. My poor dear, what a dreadful time you've had. It will work it out. I promise."

Before long Laura was in bed. She thought she would never sleep, but her mother put a drop of laudanum into her milk, and she was soon in a deep slumber. She slept well into the following morning, waking to a Christmas Eve in bright sunshine. It had been very cold overnight and when she looked from her bedroom window, she saw the frost on the trees shining in the sunlight. London suddenly looked like a fairyland. The fire in her grate was burning brightly. Her mother must have had Mary make it up. Dear Mama! Suddenly all her cares seemed to fall away. Things would work out. What had Quentin called it when he kissed her under the mistletoe? A Christmas Blessing. Yes, a blessing. That's what she felt that morning.

There was a knock at her door, and there was Mary, with a tray. "Madam says you are to have breakfast in bed and not get up till later," she said, and waited for Laura to puff up her pillows and climb back under the blankets before putting the tray over her knees.

"How delicious!" she said, seeing the fruit bread and a big pat of butter on the tray. "My favorite!"

She ate all the bread and drank two cups of tea, before lying back and closing her eyes. She did not sleep. It was more a daydream. She thought about Quentin Stapleton, his charming smile, his bright blue laughing eyes, his kindness. What did it matter if he had no money? Mama said they would manage, and they would. He was a Viscount even if he was poor, and he had the entrée everywhere. So would they. Mama would have congenial society, and she would have Quentin. That's all she wanted.

She dressed and went downstairs for lunch. Then, to her surprise, her mother announced, "I have an errand to run, so I'll be leaving you for a little while."

"But, Mama, don't you want me to come with you? Are you sure you're strong enough to go out alone?"

"I'll take Mary. She enjoys a little jaunt. You stay here. I'm still not convinced you're not coming down with something. Although you look very well today, my dear!"

"It's Christmas Eve, and a lovely sunny day, so I felt like dressing up a bit."

She was wearing a violet velvet gown that brought out the flame in her hair and contrasted beautifully with the whiteness of her skin.

"I'm glad you did," said her Mama, and gave a secret smile.

8

About an hour after her mother had left, Laura was surprised by the door knocker. Who would be calling on Christmas Eve? Mary had gone with Mrs. Wentworth, so Laura opened the door herself.

In front of her stood Quentin Stapleton, carrying a large ball of mistletoe, bedecked with ribbons. He stepped in and shut the door. Before she could say a word, he held the kissing ball above her head with one hand and drew her towards himself with the other. He kissed her until she was breathless. Then he kissed her again.

"Now let us go inside and decide when we are to be married," he said.

"But are we to be married?"

"I should give you a hint. When a woman allows you to enter her home where she is quite alone, and then kisses you passionately, it has to be assumed she is prepared to marry you. Of course, such behavior might be quite usual in India, but here in London, it is considered scandalous."

"It is scandalous in India too, but I didn't kiss you, you kissed me."

"That can easily be remedied. But you must be frozen standing out here in the hall. Let's go in by the fire and you may kiss me."

They suited the action to the word, and the next half hour was spent very pleasurably indeed.

"You know, Quentin, if we marry," said Laura a little shyly, looking up at him, "I hope you don't mind if my mother lives with us. I promise you; we are neither of us expensive, and we have been used to the strictest economy."

"But of course she may live with us, or, if she prefers, in the Dower House. We have two, one in the country and one in town. But why should you practice the strictest economy? I can afford a wife, you know."

"It's kind of you to say so, but I know you are not wealthy, you told me."

"When did I tell you such a thing?"

"In the carriage when we were talking about the Coat of Arms. You said you were a lowly Viscount and you didn't like to raise people's expectations."

Viscount Stapleton laughed. "I meant we were lowly in the sense it's not a very old family. The earliest viscounts were named in the 1400's. We are much later, not till the end of the 1600's. I don't like to raise people's expectations that we're surrounded by great antiquity. We're only just over a hundred years old. Our estate in Middlesex is relatively new—you'll see. No Tudor wings, or visits from Queen Elizabeth. But I'm glad to tell you, my love, that I am quite well-off. One hates to talk money with a lady, but you'll be better off with me than with old Nicky."

Laura sat up and clapped her hands together. "Thank goodness! Oh!" she realized what she had said, "I don't mean thank goodness you're rich. I would marry you and live in a hovel. But it makes it so much easier for my mother. She's always had to worry about money."

"Not any more. I owe her so much; I'll settle anything she wants upon her."

"You owe her?"

"Yes. She wrote me a letter this morning telling me to come and make you marry me. She said you loved me but felt a sense of responsibility to so many people it was overwhelming you. She said not to take no for an answer." He thought for a moment. "My darling, do you want me to propose properly? Down on one knee?"

"I... I think I would! I seem to have become such a romantic! Just three weeks ago I was perfectly ready to marry a man who hadn't proposed at all. I know it's silly, but would you?"

In answer, the Viscount drew Laura to her feet and then went on one knee before her.

"My dear Miss Wentworth," he said, looking up into her eyes. "Would you do me the honor of...."

But before he could finish, there was a step in the hall and the drawing room door was pushed open.

"Oh, there you are!" said Mrs. Wentworth, coming into the room, still in her pelisse and bonnet. "And Lord Stapleton. Good. I have some important news."

Quentin had risen somewhat awkwardly to his feet and now said, "Am I included in this news or should I leave you?"

"No, stay, stay," came the reply. "This concerns you, too. At least, I expect it does." She flung off her very becoming bonnet and sat down. "I am to be married," she announced firmly. "To Mr. Branson Senior."

"What? No, Mama!" cried Laura. "There's not the least need. Quentin is rich! He can provide for us both. You can even have your own house, if you want!"

"But, my dear," said her mother. "You don't understand. I wish to be married. I am not so old that I've given up on the... the company of a gentleman. I knew Mr. Branson before I married your father, and I always liked him, though he was overshadowed by your father at the time. When I went to see him today I was simply going to tell him not to be such a goose, to allow his son to marry where he liked and allow you to do the same. But when I saw him, the years fell away! I felt like a girl again. Besides, the poor man needs a wife! He simply cannot manage on his own. His melancholy and stubborn refusal of any change over the last year is proof enough of that. And it was clear he felt the same. He greeted me with such affection, and the minute we began talking it was like the old days! Anyway, it's all arranged. You shall marry your Quentin, if I may call you that?" she turned to her future son-in-law and received a smiling nod. "And I shall marry Mr. Branson. Now I'll leave you to... to finish what you were doing."

She turned to go, then turned back, "Oh, I forgot to tell you. Young Nicky is to marry Miss Thomas. It seems that this very morning he had gone boldly to his Papa and told him that even if he was cut off without a penny, he would marry where he chose. My Nicholas told me he was so surprised at that show of determination, a thing he had rarely seen from his boy, he agreed at once to the betrothal. By the time I got there, he was puffed up with pride at what he called his son's bottom. Gentlemen are so strange!" And with that she left them.

"Well!" said Laura, turning to her almost fiancé. "What an amazing outcome! Whoever would have imagined such a thing?"

"It's a Christmas blessing for us all, to be sure," smiled Quentin Stapleton, Viscount. "Now, if we may take up where we left off?"

He knelt on one knee again. "Miss Wentworth, my dear Laura...."

The End

Love
and
The Royal Society

1

"Good gracious!" said Ianthe to herself as she settled her skirts and looked around the hall. "Who would have thought so many people would be interested in a lecture about chemistry at the Royal Society?"

But so it was. Other than the one next to her, she could see no vacant seat. The fact that the one next to her had not been taken was probably because she was on the aisle. Even these days, it was rare for a woman to come alone, so people probably thought she was waiting for her companion. No single gentleman would like to ask her to stand up so he might take it.

She was accustomed to being unaccompanied on such outings. Until his death a year ago, her father had brought her with him to these lectures. He had always wanted a son to carry on his experimentation in chemistry, but after her mother died giving birth to her, he had been forced to accept that Ianthe was his only heir. He had treated her as he would have done a son, except that since she couldn't go to Harrow and Cambridge as he had done, he taught her at home. As a consequence, she could read Latin and Greek and knew the properties of the various elements he had arranged in his laboratory. She had been a willing assistant and scribe when he performed his experiments, and if her enthusiasm for the subject had been rather less than his, she never let it show.

The man she had come to see today was, she was convinced, indirectly the cause of her father's death. In 1800 Humphrey Davy had published a book on the effects of nitrous oxide, which he termed *laughing gas*. He had apparently used it with his friends Robert Southey, Samuel Taylor Coleridge and William Wordsworth, the famous Lake Poets. They had all enjoyed it immensely, with no ill effects. Davy himself had seen its possibilities as a pain reliever during surgery, but as far as Ianthe knew it never been used that way. Her father had wanted to try it and had created the gas in his laboratory. Not wishing to harm other members of the household, he had fashioned a mask for himself and fed the gas directly into it. When Ianthe had come into the laboratory to see how he was getting on, she had found him unconscious on the floor. She was able to bring him to his senses using *sal volatile* but a subsequent examination showed he had suffered a seizure. The physician declared that the gas was not the cause of the attack, but a weak heart. Ianthe had nonetheless always wondered whether being deprived of sufficient oxygen had brought it on.

He had lingered in bed for another seven days, declaring in a weak voice that he just needed rest. Towards the end of the week, however, he must have felt his time was come, for he called Ianthe to his side. He made her promise she would always look after his younger sister, her aunt Mariah, and never leave her. This lady had come to live with them after the death of Ianthe's mother and had dedicated herself to the comfort of her young niece. She played with her all day long, sat up with her during her bouts of childish ailments, soothed her fevers and read interminably from a large book of fairy stories.

It was not until she was older that Ianthe realized her aunt was in many ways little more than a child herself. She was fearful of anything new or different and had an unreasoning hatred of men. The only male she could bear was her brother. He explained to Ianthe that his sister had always been very timid and had been frightened out of her wits as a small child by the eruption into her bedchamber of a large man engaged to clean the windows. He had overbalanced from his ladder and, clutching at the window sill to prevent his falling, had then climbed into the bedroom. He had sought to calm the fears of the young occupant by approaching her, waving his dusters, and trying to explain. But he had succeeded only in making her so hysterical that by the time her screams had roused the rest of the household, she had fallen into a fit.

She had never really recovered. She had stayed at home with their parents, never marrying or even talking to any men, until she had come to live with her brother and Ianthe. Luckily, their only male servant was an elderly general factotum who was of an age where he could be pensioned off. After that, they had employed no more men.

Aunt Mariah never left the house, except to go into the garden. In the good weather she spent her time there, where she had a positive genius for roses. When it became too cold to be outside, she passed her time embroidering exquisite napkins, handkerchiefs, and tablecloths. Ianthe also had a drawer full of beautifully sewn and embroidered nightgowns and wrappers. Her aunt was a wonderful seamstress and, if shown a picture of something, could make it with unerring precision. As a result, Ianthe was always well-dressed. She was not beautiful enough to turn heads when she walked in the street, but she was certainly recognized as a gentlewoman dressed in the latest style.

A few days after exacting this promise from her, her father had died. The past year had been a difficult time. Even before then, her poor aunt had been becoming more and more vague. She sometimes didn't know what day of the week it was. Now she seemed unable to retain the knowledge that her brother had gone. Several times a day she would come into the library, where Ianthe spent a good deal of her time, looking for him and asking in her thin, reedy voice, where he had gone. In vain did Ianthe try to explain. In the end she would simply say he would be back soon, and her aunt would wander off.

Finances, too, were something of a problem. They had a quite large house to maintain and the pension her father had received died with him. After an interview with his man of business, Ianthe realized that while they had enough to live on if they were reasonably careful, they could not afford to be profligate. Their annual trips to the seaside would have to be cancelled and they would not replace the maid who had just left to get married. They would manage with just the one maid, Bridget, and Rose the cook. The basics of life they could afford. Its elegancies, they could not.

Luckily, Ianthe had never been accustomed to an elegant life. With her father, she was used to being invited to small concerts and dinner and tea parties, mostly by older couples who were his friends rather than hers. She was usually the youngest person there. She had received one or two offers of marriage from older men which she had no trouble in refusing. Marriage to a man who bored her and was probably looking for a nurse for his old age did not interest her at all. For, in spite of her unconventional upbringing and complete lack of access to the romances enjoyed by other young women of her age, Ianthe secretly nourished the idea of true love.

Since her father's death the invitations had been markedly fewer. She understood. A single woman was harder to seat at table than a couple. She did not want to be the "extra woman" for whom a gentleman would have to be found. Besides, it did not really trouble her to go less into society. She was happy in her own company, enjoyed reading the newspapers and her books, and was happy to visit on her own museums, galleries, and public events like this lecture. She just wished she had someone to discuss things with. That's when she missed her father most.

She had decided to sell the material and chemistry books from her father's laboratory. It wasn't so much the additional money, though that would be welcome. After the terrible accident, she had no desire to go in the room ever again. She was wondering how much it would cost to put an advertisement in the newspaper, and whether it would be worth it.

She was roused from her contemplation of this by the sound of a pleasant baritone.

"I beg your pardon, Madam, but may I sit in the vacant seat next to you?"

She turned her startled gaze in the direction of the voice and then had to lift her head to see the face of the person who owned it. A very tall man stood in the aisle. He wore a coat that was elegant without being ostentatious. It fit well but would not need two stalwart helpers to ease it over his shoulders, though these were, she now saw, very broad. His neckcloth was tied in an uncomplicated fashion and apart from a watch chain, his sober waistcoat bore no sign of ornamentation. He carried a caped cloak over his arm and a hat and cane in his hand. He had a pleasant face, with a lock of black hair that fell over his brow. His eyes were a piercing blue.

"I think it might be best if I simply move over," she said. "I think I will fit better than you." She smiled, stood up and sat down again one seat from the aisle.

"That is exceedingly good of you! My legs are unsuited to places such as this." The tall gentleman bowed towards her with a very engaging smile and folded himself into the seat.

"I usually try to be early but today I was held up." He looked around. "I was lucky to find a seat at all. Did your companion let you down?"

"My compan..., oh, no!" said Ianthe as she realized what he meant. "I came alone. I used to come with my father but he... he died last year." And then, not knowing quite why she did it, unless it was the pleasure of speaking to another adult who seemed an attentive listener, she told him the story of her father's death.

"And you think it was somehow connected to Davy's laughing gas?"

"Yes. He was in perfect health before. We had never heard anything about a weak heart."

"It is entirely possible. If the nitrous oxide excluded available oxygen."

"Yes, that's what I thought."

"You are familiar with chemistry, Miss...?"

"Fulton. Ianthe Fulton." She held out her hand.

The gentleman took it. "Asheton, Michael Asheton." He took her hand and held it a moment.

At that moment a hush fell on the crowd as a rather slight man of not above medium height appeared on the podium before them. He was dressed rather as a country gentleman, with a coarse wool jacket and brown breeches with dark colored stockings and heavy shoes.

Without saying a word, he placed a small white crystal in the center of a plate and, holding aloft a large clear bottle, from it poured a steam of liquid upon the crystal. Instead of flooding the plate, as the liquid touched the crystal it became as solid as the crystal itself. As Davy continued to pour, he made what looked like a large odd-shaped white sculpture. When the liquid was all used up, the chemist picked up his solid white sculpture and held it out for the audience to behold. There was a round of applause. He lit a candle, placed the white sculpture in a pan and heated it. Then, with a great flourish and to more applause, he poured the liquid from the pan back into the bottle from which it had originally come.

"Ladies and gentlemen," he said with a bow, "no! I am not Old Man Winter! I cannot at a touch turn water to ice. But I am a chemist, and what I can do is use a supersaturated solution of sodium acetate poured onto a crystal of the same compound to make it all into a solid. Furthermore, if I had given it to one of you to hold, you would have realized that it was nothing like ice. In fact it was warm."

As his assistant, introduced as Michael Faraday, cleared away the products of the last experiment, he then spoke about his work in Italy with ancient papyrus. Time and storage conditions had caused these to become stuck together and illegible, even to those who knew something of the ancient language in which they were written. He showed one such example, the characters difficult to discern and the pages in one solid mass. He placed it into a small closed glass chamber into which a greenish-yellow gas was introduced. He explained this was chlorine gas, and not dangerous in such small quantities. The papyrus began to smoke and became very yellow. A most unpleasant smell was produced. After a few minutes, he removed the papyrus with gloves and tongs, explaining that the muriatic acid produced by the chlorine and the papyrus was more dangerous. Indeed, his assistant very quickly removed the whole apparatus. With great care, Davy was able to separate the pages of the papyrus and to demonstrate that the symbols written on them were much clearer.

The last part of the presentation was devoted to a brief lecture on the chemist's most famous discovery, that of laughing gas. He regretted not being able to demonstrate it there, but spoke with wit and humorous anecdote of his experiments with his friends the Lake Poets, especially William Wordsworth, who had asked him to edit his last book of verse.

He ended by saying with great seriousness, "Though these experiments using the gas with friends have been the cause of mirth and jollity, my sincere hope is that this discovery will be proven to have much greater benefits for the good of all mankind."

This pronouncement was met with rousing applause.

When the lecture was over, a number of people, mostly women, crowded the podium. Ianthe had hoped to be amongst the first but she had to wait for the gentleman next to her to move before she could do so herself. In the event, though she waited fully half an hour to speak to the famous chemist, she was able only to exchange a few words with him. She explained what had happened to her father and her conviction about the laughing gas being to blame.

"My dear Madam," he replied gravely, "I am saddened to hear of your loss. I most sincerely hope and believe the gas was not to blame. I have personally inhaled it over long periods and am none the worse for wear. But I shall be on the alert for other such reports, you may be sure."

And with that, she had to be content. Still, she thought, if he really did keep an eye out for other reports like hers, something might be learned in the long run. Scientific progress, she knew, was rarely a straight line.

She was walking back up the aisle when she heard her name called. It was Mr. Asheton. He had been waiting for her and watched her come towards him. She was carrying her coat. He could see now that she was of average height and had a good figure. Her gown, though unostentatious, fit her very well and the color suited her. But she was obviously not a woman looking to be seen and admired.

"My carriage is outside, Miss Fulton," he announced. "May I convey you home? It has come on to rain and a hackney will be impossible to procure."

Ianthe accepted with pleasure. She had not planned to take a hackney, feeling this was one expense that could be spared. But a walk in the rain did not appeal to her at all. Besides, she felt a distinct stir of interest in Mr. Asheton. He handed her into the carriage, asked her direction and walked around to tell the driver. Then he got in the other side. Neither of them spoke at first and this gave Mr. Asheton time to observe his companion more closely. She had hair somewhere between gold and brown, lit by the amber of her rather simple but elegant gown. Her eyes, he saw when she looked up and smiled, were more gold than brown and her smile was reflected in them. Caught by it, he smiled back.

"So what did Davy have to say?" he enquired.

"Not much except he was sorry and didn't think it was a problem with the gas. He did say he'd watch for other reports of the same thing, though. But he would say that, wouldn't he? No inventor likes to think his invention killed someone."

"Yes, I suppose so." Mr. Asheton was quiet for a moment. "Have you thought of carrying on your father's experimentation? Not to kill yourself, of course! But one might try it with mice."

"No, I don't want to have anything more to do with it. I helped my father because I loved him and he had no son to do it, but honestly, I have no desire to be a chemist. In fact, I'm going to sell all the books and equipment."

"He had books on chemistry?"

"Yes, everything from Empedocles, Aristotle and Democritus to Boyle and Lavoisier. There are other less well-known writers, too. I can't remember all of them. Those are the ones I've studied."

"Good heavens! You've read all that?"

"Well, not all of it, but yes, as I told you, my father wanted a son. He would have sent him to Harrow and Cambridge like himself, but unfortunately I came along, so he taught me instead."

"I should very much like to see the books you're thinking of selling. I'd like to complete my own library. Here's my card. Why don't you send me a note when it's convenient?"

He handed her a gilt-edged card upon which was written simply:

The Lord Asheton, Mayfair, London.

"Oh!" said Ianthe, looking at it. She had been going to invite this engaging stranger in to look at the books, but now that she knew he was a lord, she felt suddenly a little overawed. But then her good sense took over. This was ridiculous! *For heaven's sake*! she said to herself, *he's just a man who likes old science books. Let him come and look!*

"If you have time, you may come now," she said. "I have nothing pressing this afternoon, if you don't."

In fact, his lordship had an appointment with his tailor, but this young woman with the golden eyes who could read Greek was a much more interesting prospect.

"As it turns out, neither do I," he said. "I should be delighted."

"There is just one thing," said Ianthe quickly, before she lost courage. "I should warn you about my aunt Mariah."

"Is she a fierce duenna with a stick to beat off young men who dare to address you?" laughed her companion.

"Not exactly," laughed Ianthe in return. "She isn't fierce and she has no stick, but she may frighten you off. You see, she positively hates men. If she sees you, she may have a fit. A man induced a fit in her years ago. Whether it would be the same now, I'm not exactly sure, as we've had no men in the house for years, except my father. She's a dear, actually, but not really of this world."

"Oh dear! I promise to be as unobtrusive as possible and to duck into a doorway should she catch sight of me. But you have no men in the house? Who carries in the coal and the like?"

Ianthe laughed at the idea of so large a man being unobtrusive. "Don't worry. If I tell her you're there, she'll stay in her room. And as for the coal, we carry it in ourselves." And seeing his raised eyebrows. "I can do it. I'm stronger than I look!"

The rest of the way was accomplished in silence, Ianthe wondering how she was going to approach the subject of money with this handsome gentleman, and the gentleman wondering at the odd combination of a fine-looking woman who could both read Greek and carry in the coal.

2

They drove past the British Museum, close to Miss Fulton's address which was in a middle-class terrace in the Bedford Square area.

"I've been going there since I was a child," she said, pointing at the facade. "It was the best playground! There are all sorts of things to hide behind! Nowadays I appreciate it for different reasons, of course! I go there at least once a week."

His lordship's interest was caught even more by this strange young woman. The socialite ladies who formed his immediate circle went to museums only when they were sure of being seen and when a particular exhibit had been declared worthy of attention. Not one would go alone with real interest in the place.

When they arrived at the address he had been given, they both mounted the steps to the front door. Then Ianthe said, "Just let me go in and warn my aunt. I want to make sure she stays away from you. I'm sorry, I hope you don't mind waiting outside a few moments."

She went inside and ran up to her aunt's room. Aunt Mariah was a tiny little woman, now in her early fifties. It was easy to see why a large man advancing on her could have frightened her almost to death.

"Aunt," said Ianthe, "a gentleman is coming in to see some of Papa's chemistry books. He will be coming up the stairs."

Her aunt hunched over, shrinking into herself. "A gentleman?" she whispered in a terrified voice. "Why is he coming? Where is your Papa?"

"Papa is out at the moment." It was easier for Ianthe to tell a white lie than continually explain that her father was dead. "But the gentleman wishes to see some of his books. But he won't bother you. He won't come anywhere near you, I promise. Look, after I leave, why don't you lock your door? Then he can't come in."

"He can't come in," repeated the poor lady.

"That's right. If you lock the door, he can't come in. I'll come up afterwards and tell you when he's gone."

"He can't come in," said her aunt again. "Lock the door. He can't come in."

"Exactly. I'm going out now. I'll wait on the other side until I hear you lock the door." Ianthe bent over her frail aunt and kissed her warmly. "I promise it will be all right. I'm going now. You lock the door. I'll wait till I hear it."

She did as she said, and waited. In a moment she heard the key turn. Then she ran lightly down the stairs.

It was most unusual for his lordship to be kept standing before a closed front door, and he felt a little foolish. He had given his driver orders to walk the horses, so he couldn't even wait in the carriage. He was glad when after a few minutes, Miss Fulton opened the door and welcomed him into the hall. He looked around for someone to take his cloak, hat, and cane, but remembered they would have no butler, so simply put them on a chair as he passed. His hostess didn't seem to notice.

She led him up two flights of stairs into what had probably been a bedchamber on the back of the house. It smelled, not unpleasantly, of a mixture of chemicals he could not name individually. Down the center was a long cabinet made of oak, with many drawers beneath. The top was loaded with different shapes and sizes of glass jars and retorts, rubber hoses, pipettes, burners, tongs, and odd shaped tools. The whole thing could have done with a good dusting. There were a couple of wooden stools and in one corner a large old armchair, faded to a color it would have been impossible to name. Next to it was a washstand with a bowl, but no pitcher. Along one wall were shelves carrying stoppered glass jars of different colored powders, liquids, and crystals. They had faded labels written in a fine, old-fashioned hand. The opposite wall bore bookshelves filled not only with books standing up or lying down, but also untidy piles of pamphlets, magazines, and other papers, together with a collection of random items that had clearly been placed there and forgotten. These included a number of pieces of rock, a broken teacup and a tarnished silver-backed gentleman's hairbrush. Like the cabinet and work surface, it was all very dusty.

"I'm sorry it's such a mess," apologized Miss Fulton. "Father didn't like anyone to clean in here. He was always afraid we'd disturb something important. And since his death, I've... I've avoided coming in. To tell you the truth, I wish I could get rid of it altogether." She hesitated for a moment then said, "Why don't you look at the books and see if anything there interests you. I'll leave you to it. I expect it will be easier not having me peering over your shoulder. Afterwards we can have a cup of tea in the drawing room. It's opposite the bottom of the stairs."

In fact, Lord Asheton would have enjoyed her company, but he judged, rightly, that being in the room upset her. It also occurred to him that she preferred not spending time alone with a man, unchaperoned, in what might have been a bedroom. But in this he was mistaken. Miss Fulton did not give it a thought.

About twenty minutes later, he came downstairs with a small pile of books in his hand. He found her in the drawing room, reading the newspaper. She leaped up when he came in.

"Oh, there you are! Oh dear! Your hands are dreadfully dirty! I should have thought to bring up some water to wash them. I think you'd best come into the kitchen. I'm going to make tea anyway."

She didn't wait for a response but led the way out of the room. Lord Asheton, who had tried to clean his hands and in doing so had probably ruined forever his large snowy handkerchief embroidered in the corner with an elegant *A*, hastily put down the books and followed her. As was usual in such homes, the kitchen was in the basement. They went down a set of uncarpeted wooden stairs into a wide, rather dark room. On one side there was a window and a stout oak door that gave out onto the front on the building. It could be accessed by wrought iron steps leading down next to the front door. Above, on the linkway, you could see the hurrying or leisurely feet of passers-by as they went on their way.

Miss Fulton greeted an apron-covered lady standing by a large deal table, mixing something in a bowl. "Hello Rose! This is... er, Mr. Asheton. He has been looking at father's books. He needs to wash his hands." She found she didn't want to use their visitor's title. He seemed so much more approachable as plain Mister.

Rose recognized Quality when she saw it and stopped mixing to bob a curtsey. Their visitor, who was unaccustomed to being introduced to the cook, gave a brief bow. He was then led to a deep sink under the window. Miss Fulton flitted to the stove and brought over a large kettle. She fitted the plug into the drain, turned on the tap and allowed cold water to flow into the sink. Then she turned it off and added hot water, feeling it with her hand.

When she was satisfied, she said, "There, that should do. I think it's warm enough. There's still enough water in the kettle for tea. I was so glad when father insisted on installing the closed stove. It was different for Rose at first, but now even she would agree how much easier it is to work with than the old open fire. I'll just put this on to re-boil and make the tea." She handed him a block of soap that smelled strongly of carbolic and a rough towel. "I'm sorry. The better soap and towels are all upstairs. I hope you can manage with this." She smiled up at him.

His lordship thought that so long as Miss Fulton smiled at him like that, he could probably manage with just about anything. He smiled back. "Thank you," he said. "I'm sure it will be perfectly satisfactory."

He finished his ablutions and said, "If I may, I'll take this towel with me to wipe off the books. I'm afraid it's already rather dirty."

Then he saw his hostess lifting up a large tray carrying cups, saucers, a teapot and hot water jug and a plate of something that looked like macaroons. He was very partial to macaroons. He strode to her, saying, "Let me take that and you take the towel." She smiled at him again, exchanged burdens with him and, for the first time in his life, his lordship carried his own tea into the drawing room.

They sat opposite each other and sipped their tea. Miss Fulton told him to please help himself to the macaroons. Since she made no attempt to hand the plate to him, he did so. They were delicious. When he commented on the fact, she replied, "Oh yes, Rose is an excellent cook. We're so lucky to have her, especially as she now has no help in the kitchen. We just have one maid to do the housework. That's why I made the tea myself. I try to save them both as much work as possible."

Once he had finished his tea and eaten as many of the macaroons as he thought was seemly, Lord Asheton picked up the books and wiped them carefully. Ianthe was just wondering how to come to the thorny subject of money when he said, "I think a reasonable price for these would be £50. There is an early copy of Empedocles and Plato's dialogue with Timaeus as well as Salernus's account of wine making."

"£50 seems an awful lot of money!" exclaimed Ianthe.

"Does it? It seems reasonable to me. These are rare volumes."

In fact, Lord Asheton had named a sum which he judged would be high enough to be of real value to Miss Fulton without embarrassing her. He doubted whether she would be able to sell them at that price elsewhere, though he would have paid twice as much if he had thought she would take it.

"Well, if you think so, thank you Mr.... my lord."

"Please call me Asheton." He smiled.

"It certainly seems better for someone who's been forced to wash his hands in the kitchen," laughed Ianthe.

They laughed together. Lord Asheton took out his pocketbook and withdrew a £50 note. He placed it on the table. They sat in silence for a minute. Then he said, "I didn't like to keep you waiting any longer today but I should like to return to look more closely. Would that be possible?"

Miss Fulton had conceived as much of a desire to see her visitor again as he had of continuing their acquaintance, so she answered, "By all means. I am at home most days, except if I take a stroll to the British Museum. I just need to warn my aunt, so please let me know when you would like to come."

"In that case, I shall come next Tuesday, five days from now, at two in the afternoon." Lord Asheton happily jettisoned whatever other plans his secretary might have made for him.

With this agreement, they both stood and Ianthe led her visitor to the front door. He recovered his belongings from the chair. She extended her hand. He took it and bent over, bringing it to his lips.

"I cannot tell you how happy I am to have met you, Miss Fulton," he said.

She nodded in agreement, feeling exactly the same, but momentarily unable to say a word.

His lordship put his hat on his head, tapped it with his cane in salutation, and walked slowly down the street. He knew his driver would find him.

Ianthe ran back upstairs to her aunt's room. "You can open the door now, Aunt. The gentleman has gone."

"Gone? He's gone? You're sure?"

"Yes. I just closed the front door behind him. He's definitely gone."

"You're sure?" her aunt insisted.

"Yes, dear. Unlock the door! You won't believe it! He paid £50 for some of the books!"

Her aunt finally unlocked the door, but shrank away from it, as if the gentleman might somehow appear. Ianthe went in and closed it firmly. "Look! A £50 bank note!" she said. "I'm going to buy you some *marrons glacés*. I know how you love them."

Her aunt clapped her hands. "*Marrons glacés!*" she said. "My favorite! I'll share them with your Papa. He likes them too."

3

The following Tuesday Ianthe told her aunt the same gentleman was coming and he might buy more books.

"But must he come? I still have nearly a whole box of marrons," said her aunt.

"I know, but if he buys more books, there may be other things we might like. I noticed some asparagus on a stand yesterday. I'll get some later. Rose will make us a sauce and we may have some for supper. Think how nice that will be! Now you lock your door again, like last time. I'll wait outside till I hear the key turn. Don't be alarmed if you hear him come up the stairs. He won't come near you. I'll be with him to make sure."

Lord Asheton turned up exactly on time and was again shown to the laboratory. This time Ianthe had put a pitcher of warm water in the laboratory so he might wash his hands. His lordship was quite disappointed; he had enjoyed washing his hands in the kitchen. It was slightly tidier in the laboratory because Ianthe had tried to do a little clearing up. But she had found the memory of her father's body on the floor so oppressive she had had to give it up.

She was surprised when he came down after only fifteen minutes, bearing two more books. "I made sure you would be longer!" she said when he came into the drawing room. "I thought you wanted to do a more complete examination."

"I found these two quite quickly and decided that was enough for today. The hunt is exciting and I don't want it over too soon."

The truth was, the books he had taken the week before were still sitting on his library table unopened, and there was nothing more on the late chemist's shelves that he didn't have. But his lordship had realized the longer he dragged out the exploration of the library, the more often he would be able to see Miss Fulton.

"Well, I haven't made the tea yet, if you don't mind waiting a few minutes."

"I'd rather accompany you to the kitchen, if you don't mind," he replied. "I'll carry the tray."

"Of course!" she smiled at him, and he smiled back.

After tea, which this week featured some small lemon tarts also much enjoyed by the visitor, Ianthe suggested they walk down to see if there was still asparagus to be had.

"Certainly. But first let me pay you for the books."

He placed £40 on the table and Ianthe picked it up.

"I'm sure you have paid me too much," she said. "You must let me buy you some asparagus."

"Not at all! Your father has a fine collection and I feel like a child in a chocolate shop, not knowing which delight to pick first. But I am very fond of asparagus. Almost as much as lemon tarts!"

They strolled companionably down the street and Ianthe found herself telling Lord Asheton about her aunt, about the shock she had endured as a small child.

"She came to look after me when my mother died and always loved me as if I were her own. She was like an older sister and mother combined. She would play with me all day and sit with me till I slept. But her understanding was never strong and as I grew up and she grew older, the positions were reversed. She became the child and I the mother. She depends on me absolutely. I promised my father I would look after her and never leave her."

He made no response, thinking it unfair that a man should exact such a promise from his daughter.

They found the asparagus seller almost at the end of his wares. Ianthe bought all he had left. Then she said they were only four women in the house including the maid, and they would not be able to eat much more than a pound or so of the vegetable, delicious as it was. He would have to take the rest of it home. His lordship took it with a solemn bow, as he might have received an honor from the Regent. When he got home, he deposited the package in the arms of his butler and directed that it be served for dinner, no matter what else might be on the menu. The whole household was astonished. When had his lordship ever bought vegetables? Didn't he know they received weekly shipments from his country estate? Only the youngest of the maids got it right.

"He's in love," she said. "Same fing 'appened to me bruvver. Made 'im ever so queer."

4

This state of affairs continued over the next few weeks. Lord Asheton would arrive, spend as little time as he could looking at the books, then appear downstairs with two or three. The cook had developed a weak spot for him and outdid herself week after week. It did her heart good, she told her sister Ivy, to see Miss Ianthe with a fine-looking man, not so high as he wouldn't carry the tray and compliment her on her baking. So Ianthe would make tea. He would eat Rose's pastries and declare they were the best thing he had eaten since the week before. Then he would put £40 or £50 on the table. They would often walk to the museum, or around Bedford Square, buy a bunch of flowers or a bag of oranges or nuts and squabble over who should pay. His lordship would arrive home with whatever Ianthe had forced upon him and think of precious little else until the following week. What the maid had said was true. He was in love.

For her part, Ianthe Fulton knew that Michael, Lord Asheton no longer came to see her because of her father's books. She had begun to suspect he took them randomly from the shelves. This was confirmed one Tuesday when she asked him what he had chosen and he had to look at the spines before he could answer. She knew, too, that she had lost her heart to him. She spent her days between elation and despair. Would he make her an offer? She could conceive of no greater joy than to be his wife, but she knew she could never leave her aunt, or make her aunt live in a place where there must always be men. She had promised her dear father and she would keep her word.

One Tuesday, as he came in the door, Lord Asheton said he would not, today, look at the books. He wanted to talk to her. No sooner were they in the drawing room than he took both her hands urgently and said, "Miss Fulton, you cannot be ignorant of my feelings these last weeks. You must know how much I love and admire you. My Tuesday afternoons with you are the center of my existence. When I leave, I think only of the time when I shall see you again. Please," he dropped to one knee and looked up at her, "please, Miss Fulton, Ianthe, will you marry me?"

Ianthe, who had been both longing for and dreading this moment, drew him to his feet. "Lord Asheton, Michael," she smiled tremulously at him, "I am truly sensible of the honor you bestow on me. I love you and if my life were my own to give, I would give it to you, with all my heart. But you know I cannot. I've told you the promise I made to my father. I cannot leave my aunt, and I can't ask her to go with me." Tears came to her eyes. "She's like a child, and I can't abandon her. She wouldn't understand. If it were only that she's fearful, I might be able to explain things to her, but her understanding is also now very weak. It's simply impossible!"

She led him to a chair and sat opposite him and was quiet for a moment. Then she lifted her head and looked directly in his eyes. "But," she said hesitating at first, then her voice growing firmer, "Michael, please forgive me for what I'm going to propose. Perhaps it will make you think any woman who could say such a thing would be an unsuitable wife for you anyway, but I am prepared to accept what I believe is called a *carte blanche*. I will become your mistress."

He started up in his chair, his eyes wide with astonishment, and would have spoken, but she held up her hand. "You see," she said desperately, "I've felt for a while that you were... that you might... that this day would come. I've been giving it a great deal of thought. I can't marry but I don't want to give up the fulfilment of really being a woman. I don't want to be a maid all my life. I feel I am only half of what I should be. You are the only man I shall ever love, so I'm asking you to do this for me. I can see you at... at night but live at home. I shall understand if you decide to marry later on, and if you no longer want me. If I should have a child, you need not worry. I shall never put any demands upon you. I shall make up some story. There is no one to gainsay me. My aunt will understand nothing and Rose will stand by me."

Michael sat back in his chair dumbfounded. Never in his wildest imagination could he have foreseen her response. He knew of her promise to her father but had not considered it a complete block to marriage. He didn't know what to say. He'd had mistresses, of course, experienced ladies, usually married and bored with their husbands. They had enjoyed each other's company and parted, with no engagement on either side. But to enter into such an arrangement with Ianthe, whom he truly loved, could he do it? But what choice did he have? He didn't want to lose her altogether. Then he told himself this would be better than nothing, and the aunt couldn't live forever. If they did this now, they could marry later, when Ianthe was free.

He answered at last, hesitating, "My dear, you've astonished me since I met you and you astonish me now. I hardly know how to respond. I love you and want to marry you. You say you love me but marriage is impossible. I cannot believe your father meant for you to give up your whole happiness to look after your aunt, but I must respect your decision. How can I say no? It's not what I want, but how can I refuse?"

They looked at each other in an uncomfortable silence until suddenly Ianthe burst out laughing. "What a pair we are! We've agreed to engage in the most intimate and, if reports are to be believed, pleasurable of relationships, and we sit here as if we're facing some sort of doom! Come on, let's make tea and see what Rose has for us today!"

She stood up. Michael took her in his arms and kissed her. "You're right," he laughed. "As for the... other thing, when shall we begin?"

"Is Thursday too soon?" Ianthe felt herself blush.

"This minute is not too soon, but for the sake of propriety, yes, let's make it Thursday."

"Propriety!" said Ianthe, beginning to laugh again. "Considering what we are planning, I'm not sure propriety enters into it!"

"Certainly it does. There are rules about this type of thing, you know. Normally I would come to your house under cover of darkness and leave the same way. We would be utterly discreet and avoid being seen together in public. Neither would mention the other's name. To all intents and purposes we would appear not to know each other. I would have to stop coming on a Tuesday."

"Oh! I hadn't thought of that," said Ianthe. That's a pity." She thought for a moment, then smiled up at him. "But it's worth it."

And so the affair began. Since his lordship could not come to Ianthe, she went to him. Or at least, he would leave his carriage on the corner and walk to her front door at eleven PM, and bring her back the same way at about four in the morning. She protested that she could go and return alone and that he need not walk to her door every time, but he just raised his eyebrows. What sort of cad did she think he was? Their union was joyful and satisfying. Michael was a skillful lover and Ianthe a quick learner. Afterwards, they would lie laughing and talking in each other's arms until the urge grew strong again, and more than once they had to scramble for her to be back before dawn.

The only thing they argued about was money. Michael said he wanted to make her an allowance. This was quite normal for one's mistress, he argued. She refused absolutely. So one Thursday night he presented her with a lovely diamond bracelet and earrings. She took one look and handed them back.

"Thank you, my darling," she said. "They're lovely, but you're such a goose! If I were to wear these, aunt would notice in a moment. That is the one area in which her understanding is not at all impaired. She still studies fashion publications and notices exactly what I wear. I told you she makes my clothes. Just the other day she announced I needed a whole new wardrobe because the waists have gone down a few inches."

"But you won't accept money and you won't accept jewelry!" he objected. "There are rules, as I told you from the outset. One of them is you must be very expensive. What's the point of my having a mistress if she won't try to ruin me?"

Ianthe laughed heartily. "The point of this mistress is that she loves you and is grateful to you for what you have helped her experience. You must admit I've become very adept at kissing." She suited the action to the word. Her lover was necessarily forced into silence.

Two days later she received the following communication.

Asheton House, Mayfair
The 21st of October 1817

Dear Miss Fulton,

Please find enclosed a draft for £5,000 in payment for the chemistry laboratory you were so kind as to sell to The Lord Asheton. Except for those items you may wish to retain, this is to include all furnishings, books and materials belonging to your late father.

I hope it will not prove inconvenient for Pickford's to be at your address on Monday, the 23rd of October at nine in the morning to remove the aforementioned equipment.

Please be assured, Madam, of his lordship's gratitude. He has long wanted to install a laboratory at his home in the country, where he hopes to beguile the summer months with experimentation.

Your most obedient servant,
Joseph Brooke, Secretary to his lordship.

Ianthe looked at the draft in astonishment. Her first impulse was to return it immediately, but then she recognized it as her lover's way of giving her what he felt he owed. How generous he was! She had told him she wished she could get rid of the laboratory. Perhaps it was true he wanted to carry out some experiments. She knew it was quite a fashionable pastime amongst the aristocracy. So she gave in.

Accordingly, when Pickford's came on Monday, having first made her aunt go into the kitchen and stay there with Rose, where she would not hear the banging of the removals and the grunts of the men, she stood back and let them take everything except the old armchair her father used to sit in while he was reading and thinking. Then she helped the maid Bridget thoroughly clean the room, and walked her aunt into it.

"Look, aunt," she said. "This is to be your sewing room. That way, you don't have to clear everything off the dining room table every time we use it. It overlooks the garden, so you can observe the progress of your roses. I shall order a cutting table for you and I know you can make new curtains and recover that old chair. You are to look in your magazines and decide what type of rug and settee you'd like. We can afford whatever you want. That gentleman has bought everything."

"The gentleman?"

"Yes, the one who used to come on Tuesdays."

"But he's not coming back? On Tuesdays?" said her aunt apprehensively.

"No. He's not coming back."

"Good, I don't want him here. Where is your Papa?"

"Papa is out at the moment. Don't worry, you will never see the gentleman. He isn't coming back," replied Ianthe.

But she was wrong.

The following Thursday, Ianthe attempted to remonstrate with her lover, first over his high-handed assumption she would sell the laboratory and second over the huge sum he had paid. She was hampered in this by the fact that as soon as she said, "Now, Michael, about the laboratory…," he took her in a firm embrace and kissed her till she was breathless.

When at last she was allowed to come up for air, he declared, "I refuse to enter into any discussion about it. The laboratory is on its way to Amperford, my estate in Hertfordshire, where my secretary will see to its disposition. If I go there in the summer, I shall don a smock and cap, and spend the long evenings thinking about you and making things that stink and explode."

"Why? Do I stink and explode?" she laughed.

"You smell delightful, but you do explode... quite often. In the nicest possible way." He kissed her again.

"You are incorrigible, but thank you, my darling. We are now positively wealthy!"

"Hmm... not if you insist on a constant diet of asparagus and *marrons glacés*," he said kissing the top of her breasts.

"But at least Rose doesn't spend a fortune on butter and eggs for your pastries anymore!" she countered.

"More's the pity. They used to be the highlight of my week. Well, almost. But," he said, "now this is." And he deftly removed the wrapper she habitually wore. It was one of those beautifully made and embroidered by her aunt, but Ianthe didn't give it a backward glance.

That night the expression of their passion lasted even longer than usual and they were late leaving Asheton House. Getting down from the carriage Ianthe almost ran to her front door, Michael with his long stride next to her. Usually he left her after she had unlocked the door and kissed him on the cheek, but today she was in such a rush that she opened the door wide while Michael was still behind her. He had on his caped cloak and tall hat, and almost filled the doorway.

To her horror, her eyes fell upon her night-gowned aunt, standing in the hall with a candle in her hand, which the draft extinguished immediately. Her aunt gave a great cry, pointed to the large, dark figure in the doorway and cried, "Oh, it's him! He's come back! Oh! he's come back!" She proceeded to shriek in increasing crescendo and then, suddenly, collapsed on the floor.

Ianthe flew to her side and began to lift her, but Michael was inside the hall in two strides. He picked the unconscious woman up as if she were a baby and said, "Which is her bedchamber?" The noise had brought Rose and Bridget up from their basement rooms, and they both stood, open-mouthed, at the sight of their mistress dressed in bonnet and pelisse at half past four in the morning, while a tall man in outdoor clothes carried the insensible body of her aunt up the stairs.

"It's all right! Go back to bed!" said Ianthe as calmly as she could. "I'll explain in the morning. I must go and take care of my aunt. She's had a shock, but I'm sure she will recover shortly."

The servants reluctantly turned back towards their quarters, and Ianthe flew upstairs. Michael had placed her aunt upon her bed and lit the candles. Her face was completely bloodless. She was whiter than the pillow on which she lay.

"Oh, thank you Michael, thank you!" said Ianthe. Then she looked up at her lover. "You'd better go. If she wakes and sees you, it will be even worse."

He nodded and moved as if to kiss her, but her whole attention was on her aunt. He dropped his hands, and murmured, "Send me a note if I can be of any assistance." Then he left.

Ianthe went to her aunt's dresser and found the *sal volatile*. She held it briefly under the nose of her aunt, who gave a slight moan and moved her head, but did not open her eyes.

"It's all right, aunt," she said softly, "it's only me. I'm here. You're perfectly safe."

There was no response, but she had the impression there was slightly more color in her aunt's cheeks. Taking her hand in her own and murmuring reassurances, she lay next to her. Before too long, dawn lit the sky and the gloomy October day began. Her aunt lay still, her eyes closed, as the clock on the landing rang the morning hours, then the early afternoon. At last, Ianthe decided she must call in the doctor. She hated to do it, for if her aunt awoke, the sight of yet another man would shock her again, but she didn't know what else to do.

The doctor arrived at about four in the afternoon. Ianthe explained her aunt's fragile condition and what had happened.

"I don't know why she was downstairs, but someone... *something* shocked her and she fell. I don't think she hit her head, and when I used the smelling salts she seemed to recover a little, but I haven't dared try it since."

The doctor listened to the lady's heart, took her pulse, examined the back of her head and her limbs.

"She doesn't appear to have any external injuries. Her heartbeat is steady, though her pulse is weak. In cases such as this, rest is the only cure. Nature must heal itself. There is nothing we can do. Try to moisten her lips with water as often as you can, and keep her warm. She may wake up in ten minutes, in ten hours, in ten days. We don't know. When, God willing, she does wake, she must be kept very quiet. There can be no more shocks to her system."

Ianthe nodded mutely and rang the bell for Rose to see the doctor to the door. She told her to come back afterwards as they would have to keep a twenty-four-hour watch on the invalid.

When Rose returned, they stepped outside the bedroom and Ianthe did her best to explain. "You may not have recognized him, but the gentleman with me last night was Lord Asheton. We had been… been to a party. I didn't tell anyone as I didn't want to alarm my aunt." Her eyes filled with tears. "Now I see the result of my dishonesty."

Whatever Rose thought about the explanation, she replied roundly, "Now, now, Miss Ianthe. It's not your fault. Why ever shouldn't a young girl like you have a bit of fun? Your aunt was bound to have another turn one day. Poor dear! She was frightened of her own shadow. Don't take on so. Now you go to your own bed and try to sleep. I declare you didn't get a wink last night. I'll send Bridget up to sit with your poor aunt while I make you something you can eat cold later on. I'll take over for a bit afterwards and then wake you up. You can stay overnight with her."

Ianthe explained about trying to keep the invalid's lips moist, and then did as she was bid. She was drained. Her body ached for sleep, but when she lay on her own bed, sleep would not come. Her conscience kept stabbing as if with a knife. *This is your fault, Ianthe. This is your fault.* Finally, from sheer exhaustion, she slept an hour or two. When Rose woke her, she tidied her hair a little and went back into her aunt's room. Rose had left her a plate of cold chicken and ham pie, but her stomach heaved when she looked at it. She sat by her aunt's bed and read to her from the fashion periodicals she liked so much, then lay down next to her and held her hand. She intended to stay awake to watch over her aunt, but she was so worn out that in a few minutes she was asleep again.

In the morning, she was awoken by a thin voice saying, "Why are you sleeping next to me, Ianthe, dear? Did you have a bad dream?"

She sat up to see her aunt, her eyes wide open, smiling at her from her pillow.

"No, aunt. You were a little under the weather yesterday. I was reading to you, then I fell asleep."

Her aunt tried to sit up. "Oh dear! I do feel so dizzy! Perhaps I'd better lie here quietly."

"Would you like a cup of tea? Are you hungry? Let me bring something up and then I can read to you some more."

"Thank you, dear, a cup of tea would be lovely. And perhaps just a little biscuit, if there is one. I'm sure your Papa would like one too."

Much relieved about her aunt, but dreading what she knew had to do, Ianthe went downstairs. If her aunt remembered nothing of the accident, there would be no need for explanations. But she had to write to Michael. After the previous awful twenty-four hours, she knew she couldn't run such a risk again. Besides, the doctor had said so. She must put an end to their liaison. She would do it this morning.

Rose was in the kitchen and glad to hear of her aunt's recovery. "She seems to remember nothing and I think it's best to leave it that way," said Ianthe. "Why remind her of the circumstances that frightened her so? I'll make sure it doesn't happen again."

She spent the next hour or so with her aunt, drinking tea and trying to chat gaily about the fashions, then, as she seemed inclined to drop off, left her to go and write the dreaded letter. She had just sat down when the front door knocker sounded. She answered it and was confronted by a liveried footman carrying a large bouquet of mixed color roses and an accompanying letter. She carried them into the drawing room and opened the letter.

Asheton House, Mayfair
The 30th of November 1817

My darling,

I hope you and your aunt have recovered from the shock you both received. I'm so sorry to have been the cause of it. You cannot know how I have wanted to return to your side. I've three times called the carriage, then sent it away. The knowledge that it might make things worse for you has prevented me.

I had these roses brought up for your aunt from the hothouses at Amperford. Perhaps it's best if you pretend they're from elsewhere. Knowing they're from the specter who caused her collapse could not help her recovery.

I shall wait for you to tell me when I may see you again. Please let it be soon, for I do not exaggerate when I say I cannot live without you.

I am forever yours,
Michael Asheton.

Ianthe crushed the letter to her bosom and cried as if her heart would break. When she could finally master herself, she went to the standish and wrote her own letter. She could barely control the shaking of her pen and it was both short and ill written. But it was the best she could do. She told the love of her life that she could never see him again.

5

Ianthe was both relieved and hurt when she received no answer to her letter and no request for a face-to-face meeting. She couldn't bear to see Michael, but she knew she would have been unable to say no, had he asked to see her. Her whole body ached for him. She forced herself to go for long walks in the dreary wet November afternoons, almost rejoicing in the painfully cold hands and feet that resulted. At least it took her mind off her persistent thoughts about the man she loved and the Thursday nights spent with him. She had no appetite and lost weight. The newspaper no longer interested her, and she found herself throwing her favorite books across the room.

Rose noticed the change in her, but her aunt was oblivious. Ianthe had given her the roses saying she had found them miraculously on a stall. They had come up from hothouses in the country. Her aunt took her at her word and loved them. She kept them in her new sewing room where they glowed in the dark afternoons. She snipped off a couple of the blooms and carefully pressed them between the pages of heavy books from the library, telling Ianthe she would make bookmarks from them. Ianthe would rather have never seen them again, so painfully did they remind her of her lost love. Christmas came and went. She had no joy in the season and was tempted to throw the bookmark given as a gift from her aunt on the fire.

In the New Year, when she came in from one of her customary long walks, Rose asked to speak to her.

"Miss Ianthe, I'm hoping you can help me and I can help you," she said. "My sister Ivy, you know her, works for a lady. A gentlewoman she is, fallen on hard times. My sister lives in and gets paid a little something to cook and clean for her. The poor old dear wasn't brought up to it and according to Ivy, she's got no more idea how to look after herself than fly. Anyway, they manage together as best they can. Now she tells me their landlord is throwing them out! After more than thirty years! Seems he's had an offer from someone who wants to take the whole place over, do it up, like. The poor lady is at her wits' end. She can't find anything she can afford, and is talking of having to let my sister go so she can spend the extra on rent."

She took a deep breath. Ianthe waited, wondering what this had to do with her.

"Well, as you know, Bridget's young man has popped the question and she's getting married next month. I've been thinking, if my sister could take Bridget's place, and her lady move in upstairs in Mr. Fulton's old room, then I'd have the help I need and you'd have help with your poor dear aunt."

It was true that since the accident, though she seemed to have no memory of it, Aunt Mariah had become very difficult about being left alone at all. As long as Ianthe was with her, she was cheerful, but if Ianthe wanted to go out, she had to ask Rose or Bridget to sit with her. Naturally, under those conditions they could get no housework done, but if she asked her aunt to sit in the kitchen, she grew querulous and complained she didn't understand why she had to be in the kitchen like a maid. This might be a solution and she wanted to help Rose's sister, but would her aunt take to someone new? And what if the other old lady was equally difficult? Ianthe felt she would go mad if she had to deal with two of them.

Finally, she arranged for Ivy and the old lady, Miss Enid Heathcott, to visit the following afternoon. The lady duly arrived and was ushered into the drawing room with Ivy, who looked just like a younger version of Rose: pleasantly round, with apple cheeks and a cheerful demeanor. Miss Heathcott was a small, thin woman, who sat with the straight back of someone told constantly by Nanny not to slump. She wore a much darned but very fine lace cap under an old bonnet that gave signs of having been re-dyed more than once. Under her worn leather gloves she had white lace mittens, also much repaired. She spoke in a pleasant though slightly trembling voice with the clear enunciation of someone well educated.

After Ivy had gone with Rose to make the tea, Miss Heathcott explained, with much hesitation, that she had stayed with her dear Papa after her mother died. Poor Papa had been much addicted to gambling. It wasn't his fault. It was in his blood. His father had been the same. She had never been fully aware of the debts he incurred, but when he died she was left with nothing but a very small annuity inherited from her mother. Ianthe fully understood it was difficult for her to talk about such personal matters with anyone, least of all a stranger, and just nodded encouragingly. Then the old lady gave her to understand she was willing to pay what was within her means for her room and board.

"We will not worry about that now," said Ianthe, who had formed a favorable opinion of Miss Heathcott. "Let's go and have tea with Aunt Mariah. She will be glad to meet you." At least, she hoped this was so.

In the event, nothing could have gone better. Miss Heathcott had obviously been informed of her aunt's condition and addressed her kindly, almost as if to a child. When aunt Mariah mentioned her brother, Ianthe's Papa, Miss Heathcott simply said he was working. They soon discovered a mutual interest in flowers, which the visitor spoke of with enthusiasm. In her present dwelling she had no garden and made do with pots on the window sills. They were soon discussing what grew best where, and Miss Heathcott expressed a fervent wish to see Miss Fulton's roses when they began to bloom. Then, noticing her visitor's darned mittens, Ianthe's aunt began to talk about sewing and lacemaking. Here, too, they had a mutual interest, and it was not long before they were both poring over the fashion illustrations, discussing the relative merits of fur tippets, lace fichus and flounced or tailored sleeves. Ianthe sat back and drank her tea in relief. Yes, this would work.

Just over a month later, the two women moved into the Fulton household and within days it was as if they had always been there. Rose and Ivy lived happily together downstairs, and if they had occasional sisterly quarrels, it was more evidence of affection than the opposite. The finances had been easily arranged. Ianthe asked her new lodger only to continue to pay Ivy. The task of companion to her aunt was payment enough for board and lodging. Since she no longer had to pay rent, Miss Heathcott increased Ivy's wages to be equal to Rose's and was still much better off than before. She had never been happier. She soon became 'dear Enid', and would spend hours in 'dear Mariah's' sewing room reading to her while she worked. It seemed Enid had a taste for romantic novels. Ianthe, who never read them herself, had never thought to buy them for her aunt. Now she saw her mistake. Enid would read and Mariah would sit, her needle suspended in mid-air, open mouthed at the dreadful fate threatening some poor maiden, and at the terrible black heart of the villain.

Mariah had declared Enid's wardrobe shockingly out of date and had begun to make gowns for her. The rightness of her decision to enlarge the household was confirmed one day when, walking past the sewing room, Ianthe heard them both giggling like schoolgirls over whether one tacked-together gown was too tight over dear Enid's derrière.

It was early spring when Ianthe received a note from Michael's secretary.

> *Asheton House, Mayfair*
> *The 12th of March 1818*
>
> *Dear Miss Fulton,*
>
> *The Lord Asheton begs you to accompany him to a lecture at the Royal Society this coming Friday. The topic is Electricity. His lordship thinks you will find it interesting.*
>
> *Unless he hears from you to the contrary, he will pick you up at two o'clock on Friday afternoon.*
>
> *Your most obedient servant,*
> *Joseph Brooke, Secretary to His Lordship*

Ianthe sat back in her chair, her heart beating. The prospect of seeing Michael after all these months both thrilled and alarmed her. Though the desperate ache she had felt at first had gone away, she thought about him every day and lay on her pillow every night with a vision of him behind her closed eyes, longing for his touch, his lips, his laugh.

But he had had his secretary send the message; he clearly expected their meeting to be purely social. There was no personal warmth: *His lordship thinks you will find it interesting.* Well, she would. Since Miss Heathcott had come to live with them, she had resumed her daily study of the newspaper and knew a good deal of experimentation was taking place with electricity. She could be impersonal, couldn't she? She sent a quick response, as it seemed churlish to say nothing at all and just wait for him to show up.

43, Adeline Place,
Bloomsbury, London
The 12th March of 1818

Dear Lord Asheton,

Miss Fulton thanks you for your kind invitation to the Royal Society lecture on Friday and is pleased to accept.

Yours sincerely,
Ianthe Fulton (Miss)

On Friday she dressed herself in her newest gown. It was made of a fine, rich green wool. Her aunt had had to take in the seams from the pattern she had previously been using. "How thin you have become, my dear!" she had said, but had otherwise not remarked on her niece's loss of weight. In late January Ianthe had bought herself a new pelisse, for her old one was not only getting shabby but positively hung off her. She had told herself sternly there was no reason to go around looking like a pauper and had also bought a new bonnet. It was an amber colored velvet and enhanced the gold of her eyes. She dressed in all her new finery, hoping Michael wouldn't see how thin and drawn she had become.

She was, of course, ready much too early and paced around in the drawing room, unable to sit still. When the knocker sounded she had to school herself not to run to the door. Her heart leaped when she saw Michael, and her blood rushed into her cheeks. As a consequence, he saw a young woman with a bloom on her face, dressed in the latest style. He had rather hoped she might be looking as wretched as he had felt the last months. But he looked just the same to her: tall, handsome, and impeccably turned out. Her attention was so fixed on him she did not notice that the carriage was a travelling chaise and there was a trunk strapped to the back.

He handed her inside and said, "Excuse me just one moment. I must talk to the groom."

A few minutes later he was by her side and they were off.

They sat in silence for some time, until his lordship took her hand and said, "You're looking very well, my love. Although now I see you're thinner. May I hope you've missed me as much as I've missed you?"

This was not the impersonal tone she had told herself she could handle. Her eyes filled with tears.

"Please don't talk like that. Don't remind me of the past." She looked at him, and the tears began to roll down her cheeks.

"The past is the only thing that has sustained me these months," he said gently. "But now I'm looking forward to the future."

"What future?" she sobbed. "Are you going to do something special?"

"Yes. I'm going to be married."

Her tears fell unchecked. So, he had found someone else. It was kind of him to take the trouble to tell her.

"I wish you every joy," she said, wiping her eyes with her screwed-up handkerchief and trying to smile.

"Oh, I've no doubt of my joy," he said. "She's a young woman I love dearly and for some time has been the only joy in my life."

For some time? She thought. Had he replaced her so quickly? She gave up trying to control her tears and wept openly.

Michael took her in his arms and held her close. "Don't cry, my love," he said gently. "You must know I mean you. I'm going to marry you."

She thought she had misheard and looked up at him. "What? What did you say?"

"You. I'm going to be married to you. Today."

She suddenly became aware that they had left the residential area of London and the horses were galloping. She struggled out of his embrace.

"What? No! Where are we going? This isn't the way to the Royal Society!"

"No, it's the way to Amperford. I'm abducting you."

"No! Stop! I didn't say I would go to Amperford!"

"Of course you didn't! No one agrees to an abduction. You must know that! But don't worry. The vicar on the estate is going to marry us. I have a special license. It's all arranged. We're going to spend a couple of weeks there and then go for an extended trip on the Continent."

"But we can't! You know we can't! My aunt!"

"She isn't happy with her new companion?"

She looked at him in astonishment. "What do you know about her new companion?"

"Only that to get hold of her, I had to buy a whole house in Islington I had no desire to own."

"You? You bought their house? How? Why? How did you know anything about it?" Ianthe could hardly get the questions out quickly enough.

"Rose. Rose told me. I went to visit her, you see. In my letter I told you I couldn't live without you, and I meant it. When you wrote to say you couldn't see me anymore, I was in despair. For weeks I went around like a thing half alive. I drank like a fish, I didn't eat, and one morning I woke up in a strange bed in a filthy place in the Tothill Sluices, not knowing how I'd got there—no it doesn't matter what the Tothill Sluices are. You're never going there. Anyway, the landlord said he'd found me drunk and knew I was a gentleman from the cut of my coat. He dragged me in and put me to bed. I'd have probably frozen to death otherwise. That was it. I told myself to stop acting like a damned fool and sort it out. I realized that it all depended on your aunt. So I asked Rose her advice. It was she who gave me the idea about her sister and the lady she looked after. She'd been worried about their situation for some time. With your maid getting married, the solution suddenly seemed obvious. I never met either of them. I just told my man of business to buy the house and throw them out."

"But what would you have done if I'd refused to take them in?"

"I'd have given them the house, wrung your neck and shot myself."

"Oh, Michael!" Ianthe threw her arms around him, "You are such a dear!"

"Because I said I'd have wrung your neck?"

"No, because you didn't give up on me. You're quite right, of course. My aunt is perfectly happy. When I told her this morning I was going out for a few hours with a gentleman and not to come into the hall when she heard the knocker, she hardly looked up at me."

Then she hesitated. "But I've only got the clothes I stand up in, not even a toothbrush!"

"What do you think I was doing when I asked you to wait a minute before we left? The groom was loading your trunk. Rose packed it this morning. I tell you, when we get back I'm doubling that woman's wages. She's worth a king's ransom!"

Ianthe sighed and snuggled back against his broad chest. "But what about the lecture on electricity? It might have been very interesting!"

"I'll show you electricity later on, my girl," responded his lordship.

"Oh good!" sighed Ianthe.

The Widow and the Gentleman

This story is dedicated to all ladies over forty, who rarely figure as the heroine of a Regency Romance.

1

It was about nine o'clock on a very stormy night in late November. Elisabeth Waring, sitting comfortably by the fire, had at first confused the sound of the door knocker with the thunder crashing overhead. The storm had seemed to remain above them for the last hour with no sign of letting up. Trowbridge, the butler, had obviously realized what it was, for she could hear voices in the hall, and a couple of minutes later he came into the drawing room bearing a card on his tray. He carefully closed the door.

"A gentleman begs a word with you, Madam. He asked at first for the man of the house, but I was forced to inform him of your widowhood. He seeks shelter from the storm." He held the tray before her.

Elisabeth picked up the card. *Fitzwilliam Brough, East India Company.*

"A gentleman?"

"Yes, Madam."

Elisabeth accepted Trowbridge's word. He had an unerring instinct, born of years of service, for who could be classified as a gentleman and who could not. No encroaching mushroom would ever get past his guard.

"Very well, have him come in, but leave the door open and do not go far."

"Of course, Madam," he replied with a bow, and left the room with the silent tread that seemed to be innate with every butler she had ever met.

When he returned it was with a middle-aged man of a little over average height, dressed with propriety in a well-fitting coat, breeches, and top boots. These all looked very wet. He did indeed exude the air of a gentleman, though his complexion showed the unmistakable signs of someone who had lived for a long time in a sunny climate. His clothing, though it fit well and was obviously from one of the finest London establishments, was not in the prevailing fashion of being so tight it took two strong men to remove the coat and boots. Given his muscular frame and broad shoulders, one could only say he had chosen well.

"Mr. Fitzwilliam Brough," intoned Trowbridge, and bowed his way out.

Elisabeth had risen and went forward to her visitor. "Elisabeth Waring," she said, holding out her hand.

"Good God!" he said.

Elisabeth was taken aback. "Whatever can you mean?" she exclaimed.

"You're the widow?"

"If you mean am I the wife of the late Philip Waring, yes I am."

"You don't look old enough to be anyone's widow," he countered.

She laughed. "Thank you. But my husband has been dead these past thirteen years and when I tell you I have a son of sixteen, you will see I am certainly old enough. It must be a trick of the light."

In fact, if one looked closely at Mrs. Waring, one could see the fine lines around her eyes and mouth, but her almost black hair dressed in braids around her head showed no sign of grey and her figure was slim. The general air she gave was almost girlish. This derived mostly from the good humor of her expression, a wayward curl escaping from her severe coiffure, and an unruly dimple that tended to leap into her cheek even when she was trying to be serious.

"But please won't you sit down and explain why your boots are quite soaked through? You can't have been out walking in this atrocious weather?"

"Unfortunately, I have. The trace of my carriage broke when the idiot of a driver put it in a water-filled rut half a mile down the road. He was absolutely terrified of the lightning and has an unreasonable fear of ghosts. He refused absolutely to walk back here, saying the goblins would get him if he stepped on the ground."

"The goblins?" Elisabeth dimpled.

"Yes, the silly fool is city born and raised and knows nothing of the country. He was complaining of the dark and seems to think there's something under every bush waiting to grab his ankles. I should have known better than to let someone in the office hire my staff for me. They're all Londoners. The rest of them seem to have completely lost their way. They were supposed to have been here earlier in the day to get the house ready, but when I got there it was deserted and I couldn't even get in out of the rain as they had the only key."

"The house?" Elisabeth was aware she was beginning to sound like a simpleton, repeating the last thing she heard.

"Yes. Upridge House. A mile down the road."

"Upridge House?" said Elisabeth and laughed. "This is ridiculous! I can't keep asking two-word questions all evening. You'd better begin at the beginning. But before you do, I understand your carriage and driver are stuck somewhere up the road?" Her visitor nodded assent. "Then I shall send someone to bring him and the horse back here. If the driver is frightened out of his wits, I can't imagine the state of the poor animal."

She walked to the door and called Trowbridge over. He had been on guard right outside the door, and had heard everything. She sent him off to bring some refreshment for their visitor and to tell one of the grooms to bring the stranded man and horse back here for the night. They would see about the carriage in the morning.

She returned to her seat by the fire and waited until Trowbridge had brought in a tray of Madeira and a plate of small cakes before continuing her interrogation.

"Please, pour for yourself," she said. "I don't drink it, and it's one thing I seem unable to do correctly. I either pour too little or too much."

"With a Madeira like this," said Mr. Brough after a sip, "it's hard to imagine too much!"

She did not answer that her husband had had much the same idea. But the result had been that after one too many of the same Madeira, he'd gone off for a ride on a mettlesome hunter and had had a fatal fall over a tricky jump.

2

"If you don't think me rudely curious," she said, once her visitor had settled himself down with a glass, "please begin at the beginning and tell me what brings you to this part of the country. I saw from your card," (and, she almost said, from your complexion), "that you are with the East India Company."

"Yes, or at least I was until six months ago when I resigned. I had been contacted by family lawyers in London to inform me that my great uncle William had died and left me his house: Upridge House in Middlesex. It has taken me these months to wind up my affairs and sail back here. I have never seen the house, indeed, I have no memory of ever seeing my great uncle. I must have done, however, for in his Will he commented that he had left me the house and property because as an infant I bit him painfully on the thumb. I must have been teething. He said I was the only one of his relatives who had ever shown honestly what I thought of him. The rest have spent years, as he put it, toad-eating him. The lawyers who had seen the house said it was a great, ramshackle old place let go to rack and ruin. They reported that the revenue from the estate, on which a groat hadn't been spent in fifty years, was hardly enough to put it to rights. They advised me to sell it."

He took another sip of his Madeira and reflectively held the glass up to the light of the fire. It glowed like a jewel. "But I don't know, I had a yen to come home and I hadn't been happy for some time with the Company's promotion of opium. No doubt it has great financial rewards but in my opinion, the toll it takes on human life isn't worth it. So I decided to retire and become a country gentleman, and here I am."

"I'm sorry to tell you your great Uncle William was not very popular in these parts. He never kept his land in order. The park around the house is a positive jungle, but he'd shoot at anyone who dared to climb over the wall or pick an apple from one of the overgrown fruit trees. He would rather the fruit rot on the ground than let anyone have any. An old couple who stayed with him until the end were left without a penny. Poor things. I think someone in the village gave them temporary shelter but heaven knows what will become of them."

"Well, they can come back to me! They've got to be better than the bunch of good-for-nothings the London office hired for me. I wonder where they are? The devil of it is, they have the only keys and all my belongings. They assured me they'd have the house all ready when I arrived, but as I told you, there was no sign of them. Place was shut up tight as a drum. I was going to drive back into the village and try to get a room for the night but then the fool broke the trace and...."

The conversation was interrupted by the sudden eruption into the room of a young man whom Mr. Brough took to be the sixteen-year-old son of the house.

"What do you think, Mama!" There was a very slight slur to his words. "There's a broken-down carriage just up the road. No sign of the horse or driver! I rode up and down a bit but didn't see anyone." He broke off as Mr. Brough rose to his feet. "Oh, I say, sir, I'm sorry. I didn't see you there. Is it your carriage?"

"Fitzwilliam Brough," said their visitor, coming forward with his hand held out. "You must be Waring. Yes, damned trace broke in a rut and your Mama was kind enough to take me in.

"Pip, that is, Philip, Waring," said the young man, shaking his hand.

"Where have you been, Pip?" said his mother. "I was getting quite worried about you out in the storm."

"Oh, I've been with a couple of chaps down in the Old Chestnut. Sheltering, of course, Mama," he added as he saw her frown. "Anyway, it's stopped raining now." He threw himself into a chair and stretched his long legs towards the fire.

It was true. While Elisabeth and the visitor had been talking, the storm had finally blown through.

Mr. Brough surveyed the young man. He was a tall slim youth with very fair hair that flopped forward on his brow. The visitor thought he must favor his late father. There certainly seemed little of his mother in him. He had the half-boy, half-man look of someone not yet quite sure who he was. And he looked as if he were hiding something. He seemed on the point of saying something to his mother but, glancing at their visitor, obviously changed his mind.

"Well," said Mr. Brough, "if it has stopped raining, I may try to ride the horse into the village. There's an inn there, you say? The Old Chestnut?"

"Yes," said Pip, "but it's no good going there. I heard the landlord say a group of Londoners had turned up. He couldn't understand a word they said at first, but once he got the gist of it, he found out they all needed rooms for the night. Something about being afraid of ghosts and not staying in… in an old house." He hesitated slightly. "Anyway, he was saying the storm had been good for business. All the rooms were taken."

"What old house?" said his mother. "The only old place around here is…."

"Upridge?" completed Mr. Brough, a question in his voice. "They must be the staff who were supposed to get the place ready for me."

"For you, sir?" Pip sounded both surprised and alarmed. "Why? Are you going to live there?"

"Yes, if I can ever get inside! The damned fools ran away with the only key. And what's this about ghosts? Don't tell me they're afraid of the goblins too."

"I... I don't know. I'm just saying what I overheard."

No one said anything for a minute, then Elisabeth stood up and rang the bell.

"Mr. Brough," she said. "I think it best if you stay here tonight. There's no point going into the village only to be turned away."

"That is most kind of you, Ma'am," answered their visitor, who had stood when she did.

"If we are to be neighbors, it's the least I can do," she said, smiling at him and dimpling unconsciously. "But I understand all your baggage is with the staff at the inn. We will have to find you some nightwear, and so on." She looked at him a little doubtfully. Her late husband, as Brough had surmised, was built along the lines of her son, tall but altogether less... broad. "I hope we can find something to fit."

When Trowbridge came in, Elisabeth asked him to have the housekeeper meet her in the blue bedroom. Mr. Brough would be staying there. He was also to give the groom a bed for the night. There was plenty of room downstairs.

"I will wish you good night, Mr. Brough," she said, holding out her hand. "We keep country hours here. Your room will be ready in an hour. We will want to light the fire and air the sheets. If you don't mind, I shall take myself to bed after seeing to it. I'll send Mrs. Simpkins the housekeeper to show you to your room when it's ready. Please make yourself at home. Ring for anything you want."

Mr. Brough took her hand and held it. "I cannot thank you enough," he said. "And to think, when that trace broke I almost made up my mind to return to London and forget all about moving to the country. What a mistake that would have been!"

The look in his dark eyes made her turn away with a blush. She pulled her hand from his and hurried towards the stairs.

3

"Do you have a billiard room, by any chance?" asked the visitor, after he and Pip sat in silence in front of the fire for a few minutes. "Or do you play cards?"

"We do have billiards, but I doubt the fire is lit in there. It might be chilly."

"No matter. I daresay we will warm up with the exertion!"

The younger man stood up and staggered a little. His sojourn in the inn had evidently not merely been for shelter. Mr. Brough thought young Pip was probably in need of a guiding hand. It was clear his mother was too fond to be a strict parent.

The billiard room retained the faint scent of cigar smoke but it seemed unlikely anyone had smoked in there for a long time. The boy showed no inclination to use the humidor, though it stood in plain view. He busied himself setting a light to the fire.

"May I?" Mr. Brough indicated the humidor.

It took the boy a second to focus on what he was talking about. "Eh? Oh, yes, of course. By all means. You heard Mama tell you to make yourself at home."

Mr. Brough opened the air-tight lid and took out a cigar. He clipped the end and took a spill from the mantle to light it.

Upstairs, still off balance from the look in her visitor's eyes and the warm clasp of his hand, Elisabeth caught the fragrance of the tobacco and breathed it in. She suddenly experienced a pang in the pit of her stomach she hadn't felt in a very long time.

The housekeeper had lit the fire in the blue bedroom and had hung the sheets on a wooden airer in front of it.

"I shall make myself ready for bed and look out something suitable for Mr. Brough to… to sleep in. By that time the sheets should have aired," she said to the housekeeper as lightly as she could.

Elisabeth walked slowly to her bedchamber at the other end of the house, thinking about that disquieting man. He was quite unlike her husband. Philip had been tall and slim, with a shock of fair hair falling in his eyes, just like their son's. She had tumbled head over heels in love with him in her first season and they had become betrothed almost at once. He would sit at her feet and read her poetry. She had found it almost unbearably romantic. When his eyes filled with tears at a particularly moving passage, she thought her heart would break with love.

It wasn't until they were married that she realized a romantic disposition made for a far better fiancé than a husband. He was improvident and careless. He forgot to pay the bills and often overlooked important engagements. Luckily, she discovered in herself a practical turn of mind and was able to take over the management of their combined fortune. She had at first to ask for help from the family man of business, for she had never seen a bank draft in her life, much less written one. Allowances and Settlements were only words to her. She had always received generous pin-money from her father but he had paid all her bills. Now she learned about quarterly payments, investments, compound interest, and how to read a financial statement.

It was good she did, for two years after Pip was born, her husband's father had died and he had succeeded to the family estates. They moved here, into the family home. The landholdings were not very extensive but it was she who managed them, again with advice, this time from the land agent. Good management together with their inheritances kept them very comfortably. Often and again, seeing her poring over the accounts, her husband would swing her to her feet and dance her around the room to a tune of his own invention. She would laugh and he would kiss her saying that though he had loved her as a girl with a posy of flowers in her hand, he loved her even more holding a pen and frowning over her sums. They were very happy.

It was perhaps inevitable that his carelessness should lead to his demise. He had enjoyed a glass of Madeira too many before lunch one day and then afterwards declared he would take one of the hunters out for a good gallop. He was familiar with the countryside and should have been paying more attention, but he took a wild jump over a hedge everyone knew had a tricky ditch on the other side. His horse had stumbled; he had fallen awkwardly and broken his neck.

Elisabeth had been bereft. She thought she would go mad with grief. It had only been the need to care for her young son, just three at the time, that had kept her sane. She had devoted herself to him entirely and they had always been very close. Even now, at sixteen, he still told her everything. As Pip had grown, she gradually re-built her life, going to genteel parties in the neighborhood, taking a house in Worthing in the summer (the excesses of Brighton not being to her taste) and occasionally going to stay with old friends for a few weeks in London for a chance to visit the museums and see the plays.

She had, of course, received numerous offers of marriage. She was a pretty woman and known to possess something of a fortune besides a fine house in the country. She had refused them all without regret. She had never felt anything like that pang of physical response to any other man, until tonight. Some of her suitors had gone so far as to find her direction in Middlesex and ride out to it in the hopes of furthering their claim. She had received them kindly, offered them tea and then rung for Trowbridge to show them the door. She loved her home and was very happy there, even when Pip, like his father before him, had gone off to Eton and she had been left alone. He was home now, supposedly studying for the Oxford entrance examination, but in reality, she knew, getting up to all sorts of silly tricks with his old friends. She smiled fondly. He was a good boy.

The good boy was downstairs in the billiard room playing very poorly, unable to keep his cue steady. "Dammit!" he said, somewhat shamefacedly. "My eye's all out this evening."

"I don't suppose the pints of home-brew you had down at the inn are helping," remarked Mr. Brough as he chalked his cue. He deftly hit his ball.

"I only had a couple," retorted Pip sulkily. "Old Richards must be putting something in his beer."

The visitor made no reply to this, but continued to win.

"Good thing we didn't play for money," said Pip at the end of the game.

"Oh, you were safe with me," said Mr. Brough, calmly. "I never bet money on a game with someone who's half cut."

"I'm not half cut!" protested Pip. "I told you I only had two tankards."

"Don't bite my nose off, young'un," said his tormentor, giving his shoulder a friendly grip. "I don't care how many you had. Nothing to do with me. I'm just telling you my scruples."

Pip didn't know how to answer. He felt small, and that, together with what was already on his conscience, made him disinclined to continue in conversation with their visitor.

"I expect your room's ready by now," he said. "I'll go and see."

But as they walked back towards the drawing room, Mrs. Simpkins came down the stairs, and with a curtsey, told Mr. Brough all was prepared for him.

"I'll wish you goodnight, then, young Pip," he said cheerfully, extending his hand to the man of the house.

Pip took it, not very graciously. "Goodnight. I hope you sleep well," he said mechanically.

Mr. Brough climbed the stairs behind the housekeeper. She was a grandmotherly type who he guessed had spent most of her life in the house and treated her employers as her children. She showed him his room, which was warm and comfortable, and told him she'd put a brick in his bed.

"For Mr. Trowbridge said as how you'd been living in India, sir," she said. "I understand it's fearful hot there. You must be feeling the cold now you're back home."

"I am indeed," he said. "I'd forgotten how miserable the weather can be at this time of the year. I've been sitting in damp boots all evening. I wonder if I can trouble you to take them away and dry them in the kitchen. Then, if someone could give them a bit of a clean in the morning?"

"Of course, sir. I believe Madam put out some dry stockings for you, along with some nightwear. Now, do you want me to call one of the footmen, or can I help you off with those boots?"

He said if she didn't mind, her help would be quite sufficient. "They're not those dammed tight things I see the dandies in London wearing," he said, as he sat in a side chair while she helped get them off. "Some of them must need a snake charmer to get their legs out."

Well, sir, I don't know as I understand what that may be, nor I don't want to, neither, if there's snakes involved." She shuddered.

He laughed. Then she pointed at the pile of linen on the bed. "Stockings are over there, sir, and there's warm water on the washstand. I hope you have a good night, sir."

"If I don't, I shall only have myself to blame. It won't be because you didn't take care of me. Thank you." He grinned at her, and she couldn't help smiling back.

"Now there's a thing," she said to herself, as she went downstairs. "I wonder...."

Fitzwilliam Brough lay comfortably in his bed also wondering. He had gone to India as a very young man, his heart broken by a pretty Miss to whom he had proposed marriage. She had preferred a man with a substantial fortune. As a younger son, he had nothing but himself and his love to offer, plus a willingness to do whatever he could to give her everything she wanted. But it hadn't been enough. At the time he thought he would never recover, but now he couldn't even remember her face. He found himself idly wondering what had become of her. He did remember that she had been pleasantly rounded, so he thought she might have become a stout matron with numerous grandchildren and a snuffling lapdog. His sense of the ridiculous, never too far from the surface, made him chuckle.

Once in India, his broken heart had found balm in hard work and a fascination with the country. One day he woke up to the knowledge that he no longer thought of his lost love every day, and before long he ceased to think of her at all. He had risen quickly in the Company and by careful husbandry and an eye for investment, had become a wealthy man. To be sure, his life had not been all work. There had been quite a succession of ladies, but none had provoked that feeling he had experienced with his first love. If he had forgotten her, he had not forgotten the shock in his heart he had experienced when he first saw her. He had decided that perhaps it only comes once in a lifetime. But tonight, when Elisabeth Waring had held out her hand with a smile, he had felt it again.

4

Mr. Brough was awakened from a very comfortable night's sleep by two maids creeping in to make up the fire. He parted the bed curtains and looked out.

"Oh sir! Beg pardon for waking you up!" said one of them. "Madam said we should be ever so quiet but to bring in 'ot water and a razor and make up the fire so's you wouldn't be cold. Mrs. Simpkins said as 'ow you're finding it chilly, being back from India where it's ever so 'ot and folks put snakes in their breeches, seemingly."

He laughed heartily. "Don't believe it! Mrs. Simpkins is funning with you. But they do put a big snake called a cobra in a basket and it goes to sleep. Then, when they play a kind of flute, it wakes up and lifts its head out. It seems to sway to the music, but I'm sure it can no more hear it than the man in the moon. But it's a fine sight. A great big snake with a wide, flat head rises up and waves around." He suited the action to the word and waved his arm like a snake, with his hand cupped like its head. The two girls screeched in delicious terror, and scuttled to the door.

"You don't 'ave one o' them snake baskets with you, do you, sir?" said one of them.

"No, they don't like the cold, so you've nothing to worry about. You can tell Mrs. Simpkins I won't be putting snakes in my breeches today or any other day!"

That seemed to relieve them. "Would you be wanting a cup of tea or choc'late, sir? We can bring it up direkly."

"Is the rest of the house up and about yet?"

"Mr. Pip is still abed, but Madam is having her breakfast."

"In that case, I shall go downstairs."

The two girls bobbed a curtsey and went off, giggling together about snakes and breeches.

About thirty minutes later, Mr. Brough padded downstairs in borrowed socks and asked to be directed to the kitchen to find his boots.

"Allow me to fetch them," said the faithful Trowbridge.

"Don't bother," he replied in his abrupt style. "I'd like to thank Mrs. Simpkins for the best night's sleep I've had since I arrived home."

He found the housekeeper and the rest of the staff entranced by the account of snake charming as recounted by the two maids he had seen that morning.

"And it rises right up and spits in 'yer eye!" announced one of them, freely embroidering and waving her arm around as Brough had done.

He laughed. "Now, now, let's not make things up!" he said, "It does rise up, but when the music stops, it goes right back to sleep."

"And a good thing, too!" announced Mrs. Simpkins, smiling at him, and looking at his stockinged feet. "No doubt you've come to fetch your boots, sir. Here they are."

"You're a treasure, Mrs. Simpkins!" said the visitor. "Thank you for looking after me so well. I slept like a baby. Can I steal you away to come and work for me?"

"Oh, no sir!" she replied with a laugh. "How could I leave Madam? She's a dear, sweet lady. And all alone," she added, meaningfully. "Such a shame she hasn't found a man to be by her side!"

"Indeed," replied Mr. Brough. "But there may still be hope." And having pulled on his boots, he left the staff in the kitchen, exchanging knowing glances.

Elisabeth Waring was sitting at the table reading the newspaper, wearing a pince-nez.

"Good morning, Mrs. Waring," he said. "I hope you slept well. I did, very well indeed." He hesitated. "And I congratulate you. I have rarely seen a woman look so well wearing a pince-nez."

She blushed and removed the eyewear. "Thank you. One of the problems of old age, I'm afraid. And yes, I did sleep well. I usually do." Her blush was as much for the fact she had lain awake for quite some time thinking about their visitor, as it was for the compliment about the pince-nez.

"Old age!" he responded with a chuckle. "You may talk that way in twenty years, perhaps. But since you don't look a day over thirty, it won't wash today, I'm afraid!"

At that moment Trowbridge came in to take his breakfast order, and the talk turned to less personal channels. Elisabeth was glad to change the subject by remarking that an article she had been reading in The Times said there was a large amount of capital floating in the market. This was apparently due to the lingering effects of the long period of war and was affecting the value of land as much as manufacturing.

"You mean I won't be able to get a good price for old uncle William's place, even if I wanted to sell? Well, that settles it. Finding the neighborhood, or at least the neighbor, so charming, I had already decided to stay. But it's always good to know there are financial inducements too." He smiled at her.

She refused to be drawn, but merely asked what he intended to do about his missing household staff and effects.

"I shall send word for them to meet me at Upridge House. Once they've unloaded and made the place habitable, I shall pay them for their labor and dismiss the lot of them. People who are afraid of ghosts have no place in my household. I imagine Mrs. Simpkins will know how to contact the old couple who used to work there, and they or she can help me find suitable help from the village. That is what the London office should have done in the first place, but no doubt they were too lazy. They will be hearing from me, I assure you." He looked so stern, she was surprised. Up till then, she had thought him the most easy-going of men.

"My goodness! You are a hard taskmaster!" she exclaimed.

"Yes, I am generally thought to be, though I think you will find people who have worked with me consider me fair."

Once breakfast was over, Mr. Brough made his bow to his hostess, said he was sure he would be seeing her soon and took himself off.

Elisabeth didn't know whether to be glad or sorry, but she was interrupted in her contemplations by her son, who came into the breakfast room shortly afterwards, exclaiming, "Has he gone?" and receiving an affirmative, said, "Good! There's something I have to tell you, Mama."

What he proceeded to tell her caused her to frown and shake her head in dismay.

5

The following day, Mr. Brough received a note from his neighbor. He had been expecting something of the sort, though not from the lady of the house. She asked if he would be so kind as to receive her at two o'clock in the afternoon. He wrote back saying he would be delighted. She arrived, having walked the mile alone from her home to his.

He exclaimed on this, as it was a grey afternoon with a cold wind. But she said, "You cannot think me such a poor creature that I would be unable to walk a mile in the winter! Besides, I like a tramp in the wind to blow the cobwebs away."

"No, I don't think you a poor creature at all, you must know that," he answered, smiling at her. "But it will be dark by four and you surely will not wish to walk back alone. Think of the goblins!"

She laughed. "I never think of the goblins! And I told my butler to send the carriage in an hour."

"I would gladly have driven you back myself, but the carriage is not yet back from the carters."

"Perhaps you won't be so kindly disposed when you hear what I have to tell you," she said seriously. "I think you may be quite cross."

"I doubt I could ever be cross with you," he said, leading her into the drawing room. While old and undoubtedly in need of refurbishment, it had obviously been cleaned and polished. It was cozy, with a large fire casting its glow over the old-fashioned dark wooden settle and armchairs. The candles had been lit, illuminating shadowy portraits hanging on the oak paneled walls.

"Oh, it looks much better in here than I had imagined," she exclaimed. "I understood your uncle lived very shabbily."

"Yes, it's not bad, is it? Luckily, the Pulsons, the old couple who used to work here, were only too glad to come back yesterday. It seems Mrs. Pulson had been dying to get her hands on this room and the main bedchamber for years. Uncle William would never let her do anything. She had those Londoners working harder than they had ever expected, to judge from their grumbling. It benefited me in two ways. First, I got a couple of clean rooms to live in and second, she'll able to tell me which, if any, of them are worth keeping on. Anyway, come and sit by the fire."

"Thank you," she said, seriously, and then looking up at him, "I have something to tell you."

"If it's that it was that son of yours and his friends who played at being ghosts and scared away my people, no need. I worked it out already. But I must say, I think the worse of him for not making a clean breast of it himself."

"Don't blame him," said the protective Mama. "I... I said I would talk to you. But how did you know?"

"I walked around all the rooms yesterday when I first arrived. It was obvious most of them were never used, and someone, Mrs. Pulson probably, had put sheets or holland covers over the furniture. There's a small parlor off to one side on the ground floor and I noticed three of the chairs were uncovered. Then I discovered the window could be opened quite easily. The catch is tricky and probably had never been properly engaged. I was curious, so went outside, and under the overgrown bushes that constitute what used to be the border to my driveway, I found white sheets with eye holes cut in them. And on the floor in the little parlor, I found this."

He handed her a silver penknife with the name *Philip Waring* engraved on the handle.

She took it and looked at it sadly. "It was my husband's," she said in a low voice. "I gave it to Pip on his fourteenth birthday. I never dreamed...."

"No, of course you didn't," Mr. Brough took her hand, and if his visitor found it a little too familiar, she said nothing. "Look," he said. "No harm done. In fact a great deal of good has come out of it. First of all, it was the reason I met you and decided to stay. But secondly, I probably would never have heard of the inestimable Pulsons if the Londoners hadn't run away. Young Pip did me a great service."

"He has run a little wild since he's been home, I know. He seems easily...," she hesitated, "easily led by the other boys in the village.

He knows better, but has no resolution, somehow." She hesitated again. "A little like his father, I'm afraid. He was a kind and loving man but also a little lacking in... firmness."

This was the first time she had spoken like this about her late husband, and was surprised to find herself doing so. What was it about her new neighbor that made her want to confide in him? She pulled her hand from his and stood up suddenly, disturbed both at her frankness and the wash of emotions his warm, firm grasp had aroused in her.

"He would have come himself to apologize of course, Mr. Brough. But I just wanted to... to explain, you know," she ended a little lamely.

He had stood up when she did and now bowed. "Of course. But may I ask you, Mrs. Waring, to tell him I had an urgent call to London and will be away for a couple of days. Say you found me on the verge of leaving and had no opportunity to speak to me. And please don't give him back the penknife just yet."

"Why not?" she asked with a frown in her eyes.

"Just a little idea I have. Something of a lesson for him. Nothing to worry about. I think you owe me that."

Her silence was tacit agreement. He said nothing more, but led her to the front door where her carriage was waiting. He helped her up the steps, bowed again and waited until the carriage had turned out of the gate before going back inside.

Elisabeth's sleep was interrupted again that night, both by the remembrance of Mr. Brough's hand in hers and by wondering what the lesson was he intended to teach Pip. He had told her not to worry, but how could she not? He had agreed with her when she called him a stern taskmaster. Poor Pip! She hoped he wasn't going to punish him severely! Pip himself had clearly been relieved the evening before when told that their new neighbor was not at home. He muttered something about seeking an interview with him as soon as he came back and then seemed to forget all about it.

Elisabeth could not forget all about it. The next morning she twice got up from her chair to go and see him again herself, then sat back down again. The third time she made up her mind. She jammed her bonnet on her head, put on her warmest cloak, and set out stoutly for Upridge House. It was still before eleven in the morning and a little early for visitors, but she didn't think Mr. Brough was the type to stand on ceremony. She just had to find out what he was planning. Pip was her son, after all.

She knocked firmly on the door but received no answer. Perhaps he really was away? But it was a big house and perhaps no one heard her, so she knocked again even more firmly and after a minute was rewarded by the sound of a loud voice complaining, "In the name of heaven, what is it this time? I just want half an hour's peace to get a bath and…."

The door was flung open and Fitzwilliam Brough stood there, clad in nothing but a piece of highly colored material tied low around his waist, reaching to just below his knees. He held a towel in his hand and had obviously just been rubbing at his wet hair with it.

She stared at him, knowing she should lower her gaze, or turn her back or something, but in truth unable to take her eyes off him. The hair on his broad muscular chest showed a good deal of grey mixed in with the black, but the thin tapering line of hair that went down towards his navel and then… well, beneath where the material was tied low around his waist, was all black. His stomach was flat, the bare legs visible below his "skirt" were covered in the same mix of hair as his chest, as were his long, lean toes. She felt her heart beating very fast and a fiery blush spread up from her chest. She tried to speak, but no words came.

"Mrs. Waring!" cried Mr. Brough, equally astonished. "I thought you were one of the servants! I banished them from the kitchen so I could take a bath—doing them the favor of not having to carry the jugs of hot water upstairs, mark you, and I've had nothing but one interruption after the other. They seem incapable of doing anything without minute instructions. The sooner they go back to London, the…." He stopped midstream. "But why am I standing here like this and you on the doorstep like that? For heaven's sake come in, come in…. Look, go into the drawing room and I'll be back in a minute."

He left her in the hall, staring after him as he ran up the stairs in his singular apparel, noting, though shocked at herself for doing so, his muscular calves and buttocks, clearly outlined as he ran. Then she turned as if in a dream and went into the drawing room. Luckily for her, it was considerably more than a minute before her neighbor reappeared, so she had time to gather her wits and calm her beating heart. When he at last returned, he was clad entirely conventionally in the attire of a country gentleman: black breeches and top boots, a finely checked skirted wool coat, a sober waistcoat and a simply tied neckcloth. He had brushed his hair forward, but as it dried it was curling slightly. He looked every inch the gentleman, but as she beheld him, Elisabeth could not rid her mind of the form that lay beneath.

He came forward and kissed her hand. "I don't know about you," he said with a smile, "but I could definitely do with a drink."

He poured them both a glass of what turned out to be sherry. Elisabeth rarely drank alcohol, and never in the middle of the day, but the receiving of the glass, taking a sip and finding somewhere to put it down gave her something to do, for which she was grateful.

Brough seemed to have completely recovered his sangfroid. "I'm sorry about that, Mrs. Waring... no, dammit, I'm going to call you Elisabeth. I can't call a woman who's seen me naked Mrs." He laughed.

"You weren't naked... quite," said Elisabeth, trying to sound as careless as he. "That was a very pretty... garment you were wearing. I imagine it came from India?"

"The *lungi*, yes. It's very comfortable in the heat. Not quite the thing for an English gentleman to be seen in, of course, but I often wore one when I was at home by myself. I always pitied the poor soldiers in their red wool coats. Fearful stuff in that climate. But the authorities put tradition before common sense. The British Army wears red wool and that's that. Ridiculous."

Elisabeth didn't know quite what to say to that, so tried to come to the point of her visit. "Mr. Brough," she began.

"Call me Fitz. All my friends do. Especially those I've entertained in a *lungi*." He twinkled at her.

"You didn't entertain me, you dashed off!" protested Elisabeth. "And now you look the perfect gentleman. But very well," as he started to protest, "I'll call you Fitz if you tell me what punishment you have in store for my poor Pip."

"Ah, that's why you came here so early! I see it all now. To try to talk me out of my evil intent. And there was I thinking you came for the pleasure of seeing me. A lot of me, as it turned out." He was teasing her now. She knew it and tried not to blush again.

"We'll draw a veil over that episode, if you don't mind," she replied.

"It was rather more than a veil. Anyway, it's the women who wear those, you know. Sometimes rather a lot of them, which they remove one by one."

"WILL YOU STOP!" cried Elisabeth, half laughing. "I'm serious… Fitz. I want to know what you are going to do to Pip. He's a good boy at bottom and…." She didn't get a chance to finish.

"A good boy doesn't hide behind his mother." She made as if to protest, and he continued quickly. "I know. He was already a little afraid of me after I took him to task that first night. He'd been drinking, you know. Not a lot, but more than he should have. And you accused me of being a stern taskmaster yesterday morning. So it's normal you wanted to protect him, as you've done all his life. You've probably discouraged him from hunting, and shooting, and even riding too hard, because of what happened to his father. Yes, I know. Mrs. Pulson told me. But don't worry. This is what I intend to do." And the plan he outlined made her laugh out loud.

"I need you to go home and tell him my trip was delayed and you've seen me after all. But you didn't dare to tell me the truth. I was still in a bad mood about my servants being frightened off and the state of the house and everything. And you don't recommend his seeing me either, until I've calmed down. Tell him before I send the servants back to London, I'm having them take all the holland covers off the furniture tomorrow and clean all the rooms. That should do the trick."

Mrs. Waring went home and faithfully conveyed this message to Pip. He looked relieved he didn't have to go over there and confront the man, but he frowned when he heard about all the covers being taken off the furniture and the rooms thoroughly cleaned. Later in the afternoon he said he was going out to meet his friends.

It was dark that night, the moon hidden by low clouds. Some time after midnight, three shadowy figures could just be discerned outside the window to the small parlor on the ground floor of Upridge House. The window slid silently up, and one by one the figures climbed in. "We'll just have to get on our hands and knees and crawl around till we find it," said Pip's voice in a whisper. I daren't light any candles. Mama said Mr. Brough was really vexed today. She didn't dare bring up… what we did. But at least he made no mention of finding my knife, so it must still be here."

The three figures dropped to their knees and began crawling around the dusty carpet. Suddenly, an eerie whispering filled the room. It seemed to come from both sides at once. "Bad… bad…," it whispered. "They're here. Here… bad… bad…." Then a ghostly greenish light shone above them, illuminating a dreadful white face. It had huge hollow eyes and a gaping mouth full of crooked teeth. "Bad… bad…." came the fearful whispering again, and the face seemed to float towards them. The three boys screamed and scrambled to their feet. They flew to the window and fought with each other to get through it. Then they could be heard running into the night.

A few minutes later a branched candelabra was lit in the center of the small parlor. It revealed a pretty lady with braids around her head laughing, while a very muscular gentleman lowered a cord suspended from the hook in the ceiling, on the end of which was a shining white-painted wooden mask.

"I saw a mask like this at a festival once in the Himalayas," said the gentleman. "It was painted, as this is, with phosphorus. It impressed me so much I bought this one, and obtained some phosphorus. I used it for years to great effect at parties. I would cover it with a veil, just like today, and draw it off at the appropriate moment. You've no idea how the ladies cling to one when they see a ghostly apparition."

"Well, don't get the idea I'm going to cling to you," said the lady with the braids tartly. Then she laughed. "Those poor boys!"

"Poor boys, my foot!" said the gentleman. "Hoist with their own petard, more like!"

"Oh, they meant no harm! Pip told me they discovered quite by chance the other day that the window opened. Of course, they shouldn't have been here at all, but they knew the place was empty. They had just climbed in when they heard the carriages arrive outside. It was Pip who had the idea to use the sheets and to frighten the people away. They had no idea who they were, of course, and he was very sorry afterwards. He used his penknife to cut eyeholes in the sheets. He didn't realize till afterwards that he'd dropped it."

"Well, you may return it with my compliments," said Fitzwilliam Brough. "And I propose hanging the mask in the hall. I've no doubt Mr. Pip will realize he's been made a fool of when he sees it. Your idea of the menacing whispering was an excellent one, my dear. It made the whole thing doubly frightening. I must be careful when we're married not to incur your displeasure. I dread to think what I may be subjected to."

"Married? Whatever can you mean?" cried Elisabeth, turning her face up to his.

"Didn't I ask you? I suppose that's because I've considered it a foregone conclusion since about five minutes after I met you. But you will, won't you?" And he bent his head and kissed her.

"But, but…," stammered Elisabeth, "I didn't… I haven't…."

"Well, I must say, things have changed in England since last I was here if a woman visits a man when he's half naked, sits with him in the dark after midnight, allows him to kiss her and after all that, has no intention of marrying him," said her tormentor. "I'm shocked!" He smiled down at her.

He led her into the drawing room, lit only by the embers of the fire and sat next to her on the sofa. He put his arm around her and Elisabeth, knowing she should protest, felt such relief at being able to lean back against a strong arm that she did not.

Brough continued. "It was love at first sight with me, you know, but if you're still hesitating, think of it this way: Pip needs a man to turn his… let's call them youthful enthusiasms, into more profitable avenues. He needs someone to teach him properly all the things you've been afraid to let him learn, and to show him the way of the world. Marry me for Pip's sake, if not for your own. But marry me."

Elisabeth thought of the last few days and her instinctive reaction to Fitzwilliam Brough. It wasn't the sort of feeling she'd had for her husband. She often felt her heart would break with the desire to protect him. Here was a man who would protect *her*, and what she experienced when she looked at him was, she admitted, a strong physical attraction. It was a different love, but yes, it *was* love. How odd, after all this time. She looked up at him, and the light from the fire was reflected in her eyes.

"Mr. Brough! Are you accustomed to just telling people what they are to do?"

"Mrs. Waring! Of course. How do you think I made my not inconsiderable fortune?" And seeing her look of disbelief, "Why? Did you think I came back from India with my pockets to let? Nothing of the sort! You will be even better off than you are now."

"I wouldn't be marrying you for your money, you must know that!" She dimpled. "Will you wear a *lungi* if we are married?"

"Of course. And I've all sorts of veils you can wear… or not. Talking of veils, with my money you'll be rich enough to get rid of those braids and have someone dress your hair so you don't look like some sort of pretty nun."

"Pretty nun?" she gasped.

He laughed. "Yes, but I like nuns! Now will you marry me or will you not?"

"Yes I will," said Elisabeth. "But be warned: I may look like a nun, but I most certainly won't act like one."

"That will be the veils off, then," said the gentleman. "Glad to hear it. That's my preferred mode. Prove it by kissing me."

And she did.

The End

Sir Robert, the Dog and the Dimple

1

"I'm sorry," came a clear, well-bred woman's voice from the parlor, "but no matter who the gentleman may be, it's impossible for me to move Miss Worthington now. You can see how poorly she is."

"But Madam," came the harassed landlord's voice from the same direction, "Sir Robert cannot be made to wait out in the hall. He is desirous of partaking of the nuncheon he bespoke."

Sir Robert, waiting in the hall with a small spaniel, not much more than a puppy, frisking by his heels, decided it was time to intervene. He walked into the parlor and there beheld a plain woman, plainly dressed, hovering over an equally plain young woman lying ashen-faced on the settle by the wall, her eyes closed.

With the good manners for which he was well-known, he bowed. But with no such reserve, the spaniel, observing opportunities for making new friends, trotted gaily up to the plain woman standing there and placed both front paws on her grey gown. Sir Robert was pleasantly surprised to see that the woman did not shriek or push her away, but rather distractedly patted the silky head.

"I'm sorry, Madam." said Sir Robert, "Molly has no discretion. She seems to think everyone and everything in the world is her friend. This personality trait, though charming in its way, rendered her useless for duck-hunting. She was convinced the birds were her playfellows. I'm taking her to my sister for the children. I could not leave her in the carriage for fear she befriend a passing squirrel and form such an attachment that she would be lost forever. Though I might have been able to bear up under the separation, my sister would never have forgiven me."

He was delighted to see a dimple peeping on the lady's cheek, though she said nothing.

"Sir Robert," the landlord bustled forward, "Miss... er, Miss..."

"Fellowes," supplied the plain lady, dimple gone. "Nicola Fellowes."

Sir Robert bowed again, but the landlord continued, "Miss Fellowes is insisting on remaining in the parlor you bespoke for your nuncheon. It seems the young lady cannot be moved."

"She is much too unwell to be moved. Anyone can see that," explained Miss Fellowes. "But Sir... er, Robert, I pray you to continue. If you can be happy eating your meal at the table, we will stay quietly over here and not disturb you in the least. You may eat with your back to us and forget we are here," she added, with a spark of humor in her tone.

Sir Robert bowed again. "Thank you, Miss Fellowes," he said. "That would seem a very sensible solution. Except for the recommendation about turning my back. I'm afraid I should be too uncomfortable to eat at all under those circumstances. Is your... er, companion asleep? If so, might you be persuaded to lunch with me? That is, unless you have eaten already?"

Nicola was still recovering from the bustle of helping her charge off the Mail Coach, holding her shoulders while she was copiously sick into the bushes at the side of the yard, almost carrying her into the parlor, calling for a glass of water and, ignoring the landlord's protests, laying her on the settle in the parlor. She had dealt with the driver of the Mail who followed her into the inn, saying vociferously he had no time to spare, and if Miss was goin' to be a-laying there, their luggage would be taken off the coach and they could take their chances with the next one. She had distractedly told him to do what he must, and their bags were now piled in one corner of the parlor, looking as sad as their contents undoubtedly were. It was only in the last few minutes that she had become aware of the delicious smells emanating from the back of the inn, reminding her she had eaten nearly nothing all day.

"Yes," she therefore responded to Sir Robert, "Irene is asleep, thank goodness. Neither of us had any idea how sick she would feel on the coach. We've neither of us travelled much before, you see. I was fine, but the poor girl very soon began to feel unwell. She held on as long as she could but when we stopped here, she said she simply had to get off. It's a good thing we did. She was fearfully sick. Anyway," she concluded, "thank you, I would be glad of a meal. Though it seems heartless to say so, I must confess I am very hungry."

Sir Robert replied with a smile, "Then I'm glad to be able to invite you to share my lunch. But I should introduce myself properly. I am Robert Heathsmith. At your service." He bowed for the third time. "And you are Miss Fellowes." She nodded and extended her hand, which he took. "Irene is your…?" He was going to say *daughter*, but now he looked at Miss Fellowes more closely, she was younger than he had at first thought. Not in her first youth, but surely not more than thirty. She was rather small and very slender. Her long, thin face was rendered horse-like by the tight braids wound in bands around her head. But now he looked at her, he saw she had fine eyebrows arched over her rather deep-set but intelligent eyes, and there was the shadow of that elusive dimple.

"My pupil," supplied Miss Fellowes. "I am her governess."

For her part, she had formed an immediate good opinion of Sir Robert when he first entered the room. Apart from his excellent manners, he was good-looking. He was tall and well dressed, though not extravagantly so. The grey wool coat that fit him to perfection had not been made by any provincial tailor, and his dark breeches were tucked into top boots that still shone, in spite of the mud splatters around the foot. His brown hair was brushed forward into what she did not know was a Stanhope Crop. He looked like what he was. A gentleman of comfortable and perhaps even prosperous means, with an estate in the country (he had talked about hunting after all), and no doubt a place in town.

But Molly had also smelled the kitchen odors and had run off to investigate. They suddenly heard a crash and a commotion accompanied by a loud, angry wail. Ears flying, Molly came running into the room with what looked like a chicken leg in her mouth, followed closely by the landlord. "The Animal has bitten the leg off the Nice Capon prepared for your nuncheon, sir," he explained. "I'm afraid my wife is having something of a Spasm as a result."

"You wretched animal! I should have let them drown you!" exclaimed Sir Robert, picking Molly up by the scruff of her neck and removing the leg from her mouth. To do her credit, the dog repaid this gross injustice by giving her master a lick on the nose, which caused Miss Fellowes' fleeting dimple to put in an appearance.

"Well, since it was my capon, bring the remains of it in and we'll eat it anyway." He placed the mangled leg on the table, and put Molly on the floor. The unrepentant dog now made every effort to leap up the table leg to retrieve her prize, but the table was too high and no chairs had as yet been placed next to it for her to scramble onto.

"You shouldn't eat chicken bones, anyway, Molly," said Miss Fellowes. "They may stick in your throat. I'll strip the flesh off for you in a minute. Now SIT DOWN!" She said the last two words in a very firm voice, which the dog responded to immediately and sat down on her plump haunches, her tongue hanging out and a smile on her face.

"Good heavens! You are the first person the dratted animal has minded," said Sir Robert.

"Years of being a governess." replied Miss Fellowes, "It gives one a voice of authority."

"Yes, indeed," said Sir Robert. "I almost sat down myself!"

He was rewarded by another glimpse of the dimple.

2

During the course of the meal that followed, Sir Robert learned the circumstances surrounding Miss Fellowes. She had been governess to the motherless 13-year-old Irene Worthington for five years, until the death of the girl's father a few months before. Irene's uncle, heir to the small family estate, was a bachelor gentleman in his forties. He had no desire to saddle himself with a girl and her governess, and had written to his sister to ask her to take them in. They were now travelling to London to their new abode, which, Miss Fellowes said, was exciting for both of them, as neither had ever been to the capital before. If Sir Robert thought it rather shabby of the relations to put two inexperienced women on the Mail rather than arranging private transportation, he said nothing.

"Evidently there is another Mail coach at five this afternoon, and I hope to find places on it. We should be in London by seven, which I hope Mrs. Fullerton will not consider too late. It is a fine summer day and the evenings will be light for a long time. My only fear is that poor Irene may be unwell again and then I don't know what we shall do."

She did not want to tell this comparative stranger they really did not have the funds to stay anywhere overnight, or even, come to that, to pay for two more Mail tickets if the driver refused to honor the ones they had already bought.

They had almost finished nuncheon when Irene awoke. She sat up and looked around her, a little dazed. Her governess immediately went to her, followed by Molly, who was hopeful of making another new friend.

"Oh, what a sweet little dog!" said Irene. "Whose is it?"

"Molly belongs to this gentleman who has allowed us to share his parlor," explained Nicola. "Sir Robert, this is Irene Worthington."

Irene stood up on shaky legs and attempted a curtsey, but was forced to sit down again. "Oh, I feel a little dizzy," she said.

"Let me bring you a cup of tea," said Nicola. "There's still some left in the pot and the water is hot."

She poured a cup into which she stirred a generous amount of sugar, and gave it to the girl. Irene drank it gratefully. Molly had scrambled onto her lap, and she sat stroking the dog's long silky ears. When she had finished, she looked up saying, "I do feel a little better now, but oh, Nicola, I don't think I can bear to get inside another stuffy Mail coach. Do you think they would let me sit up next to the driver? There were young men up there before, so I know one may travel that way. If I can just be in the open air, I think I won't feel so sick."

Miss Fellowes frowned and opened her mouth to answer, but was cut off by Sir Robert who said, "If I may, I think I can provide a better solution. I am driving my curricle. It is fully open air and while not really built for three people, you ladies are slim enough to only count for one. Of course, Molly will probably object to giving up her place, but it may be possible to persuade her to sit on one or other of your laps."

Since the animal in question was presently stretched out on Irene's lap with a look of ecstasy on her face as the girl stroked her tummy, that comment caused another peep of the governess's dimple.

Like Miss Fellowes, Sir Robert was alarmed at the idea of a girl riding aloft on the Mail coach. Even if she were permitted to do so, the company would be entirely unsuitable, being made up of young men as free with their speech as with their manners. Besides, he was doubtful they would even obtain places on the coach. He knew it was very booked up, particularly in the summer months. The idea of leaving these two albeit unprepossessing gentlewomen at the inn with their way to London very uncertain was anathema to him. He was, after all, a gentleman.

So it was that less than an hour later, the three companions were merrily bowling up the road to London. Cheered by the prospect of driving in the open air with the sweet little dog on her lap, Irene had been persuaded to swallow a piece of bread and another cup of tea. She was feeling very much more lively by the time they climbed into Sir Robert's well sprung curricle. Miss Fellowes tied her dowdy bonnet securely under her chin and wrapped her shawl around her head. She urged Irene to do the same, saying the dust was bound to be considerable on a long trip in an open vehicle in the summer. Sir Robert had donned a many-caped cloak and his curly-brimmed beaver and sat erect in the driving seat, barely twitching the reins from time to time but in complete control of the perfectly matched pair of greys drawing the vehicle.

3

Driving his horses at a comfortable trot, Sir Robert was able to ascertain the address of the aunt in London. It was, he realized with his superior knowledge of the city, situated in a rather less than fashionable area. Irene chattered happily along the way, commenting on the sights: a farmer leading an absolutely enormous pig, cottages with brilliant displays of summer flowers in their tiny front gardens, a peddler pulling a cart aflutter with ribbons and twirling paper windmills. She seemed to have recovered completely from her sickness and even began to speak of being hungry. When Sir Robert offered to stop, both women refused, saying they were sure Aunt Fullerton would have dinner for them and they didn't want to delay their arrival any further.

However, when they arrived at the address, in a rather narrow street from which all sunlight seemed to be excluded, they found no one at home. The knocker was off the door and all the windows closely shuttered. Miss Fellowes was at a loss. She was sure Irene's uncle had written to his sister. Mrs. Fullerton knew they were coming! How very odd! It was to be hoped nothing dreadful had happened to the family!

It was only when Sir Robert inquired delicately whether they had seen Mrs. Fullerton's answer to her brother's missive, they admitted that neither of them had. They realized at last that Uncle must have simply assumed it was all right and allowed them to depart. He was no doubt glad to be rid of them, thought Sir Robert. Out of sight, out of mind.

The problem now presented itself as to what should be done with the ladies. Luckily, unlike Irene's uncle, Sir Robert had a sister of whom he was very sure. He knew if he asked for a favor, she would gladly do it for him.

He said to Miss Fellowes, "I am perfectly sure my sister will be glad to house you until we can find out what has become of Miss Worthington's relations. I propose taking you there now. I have to go there anyway," he added, by way of inducement, "because that's where I'm taking Molly. My sister saw the silly thing last time she was in the country and took a fancy to her. We were hoping she would grow into a better retriever, but it was hopeless. She's no good for hunting, and God knows I don't need any more dogs around the house."

Miss Fellowes hardly knew how to answer, but the evening was drawing in and they had nowhere to go and very little money to pay for lodging. The offer seemed a godsend. She thanked him and accepted.

The part of town into which they were now driven was, even to their untrained eyes, very much better than where they had just been. The streets were wider, the homes larger and the setting sun threw a golden glow over it all.

The minute they entered the house, however, the glow was swallowed up in the chaos that confronted them. Sir Robert's sister was introduced as Mrs. Prestwick, or Lady Cynthia to use her birth title. She was a tall, beautiful woman, but as untidy as her brother was neat. Her hair fell from its pins, her lovely Norwich shawl trailed behind her, and her children, of whom there seemed an inordinate number, clung to her skirts in spite of the clucking of a harassed-looking woman, somewhat more than middle-aged, referred to as Nanny.

The house, which was of graceful proportions and boasted fireplaces and friezes Miss Fellowes instantly recognized as the work of the Adams brothers, was fearfully untidy. There were open books on every surface, some pushed to the floor, and toys everywhere. She found herself picking her way through toy soldiers, a miniature pull-along carriage, a horse on wheels, a top without its string abandoned on a pile of stockings, hoops, canes, and an innumerable quantity of colorful wooden blocks. Molly immediately found an unidentifiable wooden animal under the round table in the middle of the room and began to chew on it.

"Dreadful, isn't it?" said the lady of the house cheerfully. "We used to try to clear it up but it was the same at the end of every day, so in the end we gave up!"

Lady Cynthia seemed in no way discomposed by having two unknown females, and one a mere governess, thrust upon her. She gave her brother a hearty kiss on the cheek, and having listened to his explanation about the visitors, she held out her hands to them.

"Miss Fellowes, Miss Worthington!" she said. "You're welcome to stay here as long as you can stand it. Robert can usually only manage about an hour, but the children all adore him nonetheless."

It was true. Nicola was now able to count them, and although at first it had seemed a positive crowd, there were only four. They had abandoned their mother and were swarming up Sir Robert's elegantly clad legs or hanging onto his hands. He laughed and swung one under each arm and, with the other two still clinging to his breeches, he stalked forward, threatening fiercely that he was their wicked uncle and he was going to dump them all in the kitchen sink. They shrieked and squirmed until he piled them in a heap on the already encumbered sofa and made as if to sit on them.

"Goodness!" said Nicola, hardly able to talk over the din. "What ages are your children? They all look about the same size!"

"I know!" laughed her hostess. "I was foolish enough to have two pairs of twins within a year of each other. All boys! Three and four years old! I don't know what wickedness I committed that I should be punished so!" She laughed again, then called to her brother, "Robert! Stop playing with the children. It's past their bedtime already. Help me take them upstairs. Nanny can't manage by herself."

"Playing?" responded her brother. "They were trying to kill me, the little devils. But I'm The Big Bad Wolf and I'm going to Eat Them Up!" He grabbed randomly at little limbs and pretended to eat them.

"Robert! You're as bad as they are. Stop it now!"

She marched over to the sofa, pulled her brother to his feet, thrust two of the children at him, took a firm hold of the hands of the other two and walked swiftly towards the stairs.

Then she stopped and said, "Miss Fellowes and Miss Worthington, why don't you come up with us. You will certainly need to wash the dust of travel off. But pray don't change for dinner. Robert cannot and my husband will probably not think about it at all."

The two ladies followed the reluctant children and the determined adults upstairs. Having deposited her pair with Nanny and Sir Robert, Lady Cynthia showed them to a pleasant bedchamber at the back of the house where their bags had been rather unceremoniously dumped. Neither of the visitors had an extensive wardrobe, so it took them very little time to shake out their two or three gowns and hang them up. They were very crumpled, so it was as well they did not have to change for dinner. They washed their hands and saw to their hair, at least, Irene saw to hers. Miss Fellowes' plaits remained tightly wound around her head and had not moved an inch.

4

It was still quiet when Nicola and Irene went downstairs. To be sure, they could still hear the occasional thud of little feet overhead but the salon gave the sad impression of a circus from which all the performers and audience had left.

"Why don't you place all the toys over there in the corner, and I'll tidy up the books," said Nicola. "It seems the least we can do."

When Sir Robert and Lady Cynthia reappeared, the salon was almost in order. At least, no one was in danger of turning an ankle by walking on an abandoned wooden block. Molly had fallen asleep under the round table, upon which neat piles of books were now arranged.

"Good Lord," said Sir Robert. "It looks almost habitable in here. It must be your work, Miss Fellowes, and yours, Miss Worthington. But I assure you, you will quickly tire of trying to sort out this household!"

"It was quite interesting," said Miss Fellowes. She had been surprised to see that more than half the books were tomes dealing with mathematics. Now this was a subject Miss Fellowes had always had a keen interest in, though it was not something she usually talked about. As a governess, it was bad enough being thought a bluestocking without compounding the image by an unnatural interest in that masculine pursuit.

The explanation for the books was soon forthcoming. A gentleman suddenly appeared in the doorway. He would have been very handsome except for a vague expression and a pince-nez askew on the end of his nose, making him look rather comical. He was as untidy as his wife. His coat was buttoned incorrectly and his neck cloth was hanging down on one side if it had been pulled from his throat by an angry hand. He certainly was not dressed for dinner.

"Have I missed them?" he enquired. "Have they gone?" He was carrying an open book clearly showing pages of mathematical formulae. He put it down absentmindedly on one of the recently cleared surfaces. Miss Fellowes instantly understood not only the source of the books but also a good portion of the general disorder.

He seemed not to notice the visitors, but peering myopically at Molly asleep under the table said, "What's that?"

"The dear little puppy we saw last time we were at Mallows, dear," answered Lady Cynthia. "Robert brought her for the children. And he has brought Miss Fellowes and Miss Worthington to stay with us." She indicated the ladies who stood up. "My husband, Mr. Prestwick." The gentleman bowed vaguely to the visitors and seemed to find it no more surprising that two unknown ladies should have come to stay for an indefinite period than that there was a puppy asleep under the table.

"Are the children asleep?" he asked. "I meant to come in to see them before they went to bed, but I forgot."

"I should leave it a few minutes before you go up, dear, until they are really asleep," said his wife. "You can give them a kiss then.

We don't want them waking up. Robert made them so excited it was hard to get them to lie down."

"How can you say I excited them, Cynthia, when you know I only have to come in the door for them to swarm all over me like ants on a sugar loaf," protested her brother. "I am the one who needs to lie down! It's worse than twelve rounds at Gentleman Jackson's!"

Since all the women had seen him pretending to be the Big Bad Wolf, his words were met with laughing disbelief. Miss Fellowes looked down and her dimple peeped. Miss Wentworth laughed openly.

"Come here, my dear, you are dreadfully untidy," said Lady Cynthia to her husband. This would have been ironic coming from a woman whose gown was awry from the pulling of her children and whose coiffure had now come completely loose from its pins, except for the tender way she rebuttoned her husband's coat, righted his pince-nez and rewound his neckcloth. When this was done she smoothed his ruffled hair and kissed his cheek. He took her hand and brought it to his lips. They were obviously a loving couple.

The butler came into the room at that moment carrying a tray and glasses. "Thank God!" said Sir Robert. "If I don't have something to revive me soon, you'll find me lying under the table with the dog!"

All the adults took a glass of sherry. Irene would have done so too, until she was dissuaded by a slight frown and a shake of the head from her governess.

"Bring Miss Worthington a glass of ratafia, Coombe," said Sir Robert, who saw the look and Irene's disappointment.

In due course the assembled company was invited into the dining room for dinner. Irene was delighted to be included with the adults, and went smilingly to the table with Sir Robert, who took one invited lady on each arm. Their host, who should by rights have performed this office, appeared lost in his own thoughts and it was only the pressure of his wife's arm on his that seemed to propel him in the right direction.

The dining room was surprisingly neat. This was explained by Lady Cynthia who said they had taken to locking the door after the four-year-olds had decided on a race that involved leaping from chair to chair on either side of the table. All might have been well except that one of them had slipped and fallen on his chin and bitten his tongue. He had broken two chairs at the same time, but that was by-the-by, everyone agreed. The poor little boy had spoken with a lisp for months, but fortunately the cut seemed to have healed well.

Dinner was a pleasant meal, mostly due to the brother and sister, who chaffed each other with great good humor. Entertainment of a sort was also provided by Molly, who woke up full of frisk and barreled into the dining room vociferously demanding to be included in the party. To encourage her patrons, she made repeated leaps up the table legs and almost succeeded in getting the tablecloth in her teeth and pulling everything off on top of herself. Miss Fellowes told her sternly to SIT DOWN, which, once again, she did. Sir Robert then handed the puppy over to the butler and told him to take her to the kitchen, feed her, then put her out in the back of the house where she could run free. In common with most London houses of its type, the Prestwick home had a walled back garden that would provide ample space for exploration by a small dog.

Mr. Harold Prestwick, or Harry, as his family called him, seemed to be mostly in a world of his own and usually had to be addressed at least twice on most subjects until Miss Fellowes quietly asked him which field of mathematics he was engaged in studying. Then he waxed eloquent on the writing of Carl Friedrich Gauss which perhaps she had heard of?

As a matter of fact, she had heard of him and said, "Oh, he's the man who found a clever way to add up a series of numbers. He noticed that if you take the numbers from 1 to 100 and split them into two rows, 1 to 50 and 100 to 51, when you add each pair vertically you always get 101! Since there are 50 pairs, the sum of all the numbers is just 50 times 101, or 5050. So he concluded that if the series of numbers is moving evenly, you can get the average value by adding the first and last number, and dividing by two. Then you multiply that by the count to get the sum of all the numbers."

That opened the floodgates of a discourse between them of which no one else at the table understood more than one word in ten, and indeed left them open-mouthed, until Lady Cynthia tapped her glass and said, "I think it's time the ladies left the gentlemen to their port. Even then, Harry Prestwick stood up and would have followed Nicola, to whom he was still fervently talking, had his wife not pressed him back into his seat, with a firm, "That's enough, dear!"

The evening ended quite soon after the gentlemen came in from their port. Their host was laughing at something Sir Robert had said, causing Miss Fellowes to think, again, what a very attractive man their savior was. Seeing him come into the salon, she experienced a thrill quite unlike any she had previously felt in her chaste existence.

The travelers were all tired, and the lady of the house exhausted from the demands of motherhood, so they said early goodnights. Sir Robert drove home, thinking how extraordinary it was that a plain country governess should talk so knowledgeably about mathematics. And then there was that dimple. When she was animated, as she had been at dinner, it put in appearances as unexpected as they were fascinating. For her part, lying in bed unable to dismiss him from her mind, the object of her musings found her heart making unaccustomed leaps whenever she thought of his handsome person and still more, his laughing face.

5

The ladies had to wait so long for hot water the next morning, they feared they must have missed breakfast. Irene still had the healthy appetite of the young and had to be shushed from announcing how starving she was as they walked downstairs. They need not have worried. Their hostess was herself only just sitting down. The household was always at sixes-and-sevens in the morning, she said, after enquiring after their overnight comfort.

"Getting the children washed, dressed and fed in the morning is a job for three or four people and breakfast is often delayed. Then Nanny and two of the maids usually take them all for a long walk and I enjoy a quiet cup of tea. I recommend you do the same. The peace doesn't last long. Today they took Molly as well. Heaven help them! My husband doesn't usually put in an appearance until lunch. He often works all night. He says it's the only time he can hear himself think."

Sure enough, by the time the ladies had finished breakfast, the children and Molly were all tumbling into the house, completely ignoring the gentle remonstrations of Nanny.

"She is a dear, but quite hopeless with them, I'm afraid," confided Lady Cynthia to Miss Fellowes quietly, "But she's been with the family so long and is so devoted to us all, I cannot possibly pension her off. I talked about hiring a younger second Nanny to help her, but she looked so distraught at the idea, I gave it up. But they'll have a tutor in a year or so, and then they'll be off to Eton."

Looking at the boys, all rolling around like puppies, with the real puppy in the midst of them, it hardly seemed possible that in so few years they would be at boarding school. It brought home to Nicola that in very little time Irene would no longer need her, either. What would become of her then? She had the confused thought that if only Sir Robert's nephews had been girls, she might have been engaged as a governess for them. He seemed genuinely attached to his sister and her family, and that would have afforded opportunities to see him. How pleasant that would have been! She allowed herself to dream.

As the morning progressed, it appeared that Irene had a talent for entertaining the boys. She sat on the floor with them, patiently helping them put the soldiers in and out of the little pull-along carriage, building arches and bridges with the blocks for the wooden horse and carriage to go under, and inevitably knock down, to everyone's intense delight. Molly was especially good at the knocking down part, until exhausted, she again fell asleep under the table.

Then it was the children's meal time. Nanny and a maid came to bear them off for their dinner and a nap. But first, Irene had the children put the toys back in the corner where they had come from.

"The horse and the soldiers need to rest, like Molly. We can't leave them in the middle of the floor!" she said. "Someone might walk on them and wake them up!" They agreed that would be very bad, and complied willingly enough.

After lunch, Nicola decided she had best write a letter to Irene's aunt in London and uncle back home, to explain where they were. She had no idea what she and Irene would do if Mrs. Fullerton was away from the capital for an extended period. She knew they were not welcome back with her uncle, and she could hardly expect Lady Cynthia to house them indefinitely.

Sir Robert arrived in the middle of the afternoon and gladly franked the letters the governess had written. "I drove past the house again before coming here," he said, "but there was still no sign of life. Luckily, a maidservant was shaking a rug out of one of the other front doors and it seems she is very friendly with the maid from the Fullerton household. She was able to tell me that they had gone away for their annual month by the sea. They won't be back for another two weeks. I fear they never received the letter saying you were coming."

"Two weeks!" exclaimed Nicola. "Whatever shall we do in the meantime?"

"Why, stay here, of course," smiled Lady Cynthia. "Irene is so good with the children that it's a positive holiday for me, and Harry will be dying to pick up the conversation he was forced to break off with you, my dear. It's so rare he has someone to talk to about his work. I understand nothing of it. Please do say you'll stay!"

So in spite of Nicola's expressed fears they would be an added burden, it was easily arranged. She and Irene fell into the relaxed ways of the household and were happier than they had ever been. Irene accompanied Nanny on the walks with the children in the mornings and played or read with them in the afternoons, either inside or out in the garden. Molly would join in with enthusiasm, though, as the older twins complained, she just didn't understand! No matter how many times it was explained to her, she could not be made to realize that running away with the building blocks was not helpful, and burying the ball under the bushes in the garden was not conducive to playing cricket. The younger twins often didn't understand either, and saw no problem.

As for Nicola, as soon as he saw her, Harry Prestwick would bear her off to his study and show her whatever it was he was working on. She did not always understand it at first, but her quick mind and instinctive grasp of the subject made her a useful sounding board.

Sir Robert came to see them every day, sometimes for only an hour, sometimes for dinner.

"'Pon my word, Robert," said his sister with a twinkle one day, "We were not used to see you so often! What can be bringing you here every day? Don't tell me you miss your nephews!"

"No," replied her brother, with a similar twinkle, "I'm never so happy as when they are outside and ignorant of my presence. It's Molly. I have to assure myself she is being well looked after. In a household like this I'm afraid someone will forget to feed her."

This made his sister laugh and Miss Fellowes' dimple put in an appearance, for Molly had become a positive scourge in the kitchens and knew perfectly well how to feed herself. When accosted by Cook for having stolen and hidden under the rush matting the bones she was keeping to make broth for the children, the puppy would flatten her ears and adopt the woeful expression of the falsely accused. More often than not, she would come away with another choice titbit and the words "Go on then, you silly little thing! There's no harm in you, after all!"

In a word, everyone was happy: Molly did what she liked and got away with it, Sir Robert enjoyed provoking the elusive dimple, Nicola was content just to be in his presence, Irene loved the children and Lady Cynthia enjoyed longer moments of peace and quiet. Even Mr. Prestwick, who normally noticed nothing, was pleased to have a kindred spirit to talk to.

6

His sister knew, and Sir Robert was finding it harder and harder to deny to himself, that the real reason for his coming so often to the house was his infatuation with Nicola. Or rather Nicola's dimple. He had worked out that this elusive delight was produced when its owner was trying to swallow a smile or was keenly interested in the topic of conversation and trying to hold herself back from breaking into it. In the company she now kept, between Sir Robert's joking and Mr. Prestwick's earnest explanations of fascinating mathematical phenomena, the dimple appeared more than it ever had before in its owner's life.

Lady Cynthia had been beginning to despair of her very eligible brother ever finding a wife. He had been seen in the company of a number of women over the years, but never one who had lasted more than a month or two. They bored him, he said. Yes, of course they were pretty, but what then? It was such a pity, thought his sister. He would make a wonderful husband and father. But it was a surprise to her when she first realized his fascination with Miss Fellowes. On the face of it, the governess had little to recommend her. She was really very plain and her gowns were hideous. But after a week in her company, Lady Cynthia had learned to appreciate Nicola's gentle dignity and quiet sense of humor. She was, moreover, well-bred. She was the daughter of a country vicar, who had himself overseen her education. He and his wife had been killed when a run-away horse had overturned their carriage and Nicola had been forced to seek employment. No, she was not good-looking, she needed to be better dressed and have a new coiffure. But she had a certain something. And there was that dimple. It was her one beauty, but it was a beauty, after all, that was permanent.

Seeing her one morning before she had plaited her hair in its usual tight bands, Lady Cynthia encouraged Miss Fellowes to leave off her braids and tie her hair more becomingly at the nape of her neck. It turned out that her soft brown hair curled when released from its confinement, and the curls had the effect of softening her long, thin face. Much better, thought her ladyship, wishing she was on close enough terms to the governess to offer her a better gown. But still, with those newly released curls and that dimple... well, one never knew.

Nicola, of course, had been in love with Sir Robert from the moment she saw him. It took her about a week to realize it, but when her heart simply refused to behave itself, she recognized it for what it was. She chided herself for her stupidity. What would a man like him want with a woman like her? The answer was clear. Nothing.

She tried staying away from the salon when she heard his voice, but for some unaccountable reason he always seemed to find her. If she was in Mr. Prestwick's study, he had something he wished to say to his brother-in-law, if she was in the back garden, he wanted to play cricket with the children. Once he even found her in the kitchen where she was shelling peas. His excuse was he was looking for Molly, though the dog could be clearly heard barking in the back garden. In no way discomposed, he sat down and helped her with the peas.

Convinced this was nothing but kindness, Miss Fellowes tried not to raise a face of joy every time he addressed her, but to efface herself and not join too much in the conversation, particularly at dinner. But these were precisely the circumstances that brought forth the dimple. Sir Robert found himself more and more fascinated. And she'd done something to her hair, hadn't she? How pretty those curls were! He found he had to force himself to take his eyes off her.

Lady Cynthia might be untidy and a poor housekeeper, but she had a kind heart and was by no means stupid. She saw what was happening. Wanting to bring things to a head, she took matters into her own hands. One afternoon, Sir Robert arrived to find the salon deserted and the house strangely quiet. He was not to know his sister had asked Irene to help Nanny take the children to the park, and had called her husband into the garden on the pretext she had something she wished to discuss with him. Mr. Prestwick had protested that he and Nicola were looking for a proof he just knew he had seen in one of his books, but she said she was sure Nicola could find it better on her own without him getting in the way.

Sir Robert had begun to walk towards the study when he heard a crash and a cry. He ran the rest of the way and beheld Nicola suspended by her fingers from one of the top bookshelves. She had been looking for the volume Mr. Prestwick wanted, and thought she could see it on a high shelf. She had to use the library ladder. Both the wheels of the ladder had stops on them, but it was the lazy habit to engage only one. Apparently this had given way, or been imperfectly locked, and when Nicola had reached for a book on the high shelf, she had inadvertently pushed the ladder away. The stop had disengaged, the ladder had come off its track and fallen to the ground, leaving her hanging.

Sir Robert ran over and grasped her around her knees. "Let go, Miss Fellowes, I have you safe," he said. She seemed reluctant, and he repeated, "I have you. I won't drop you. Let go."

Her heart beating so hard she was sure he could hear it, so Nicola did as he bade her and let go. He took her slight weight, which was no more than he could easily manage, and allowed the full length of her body to slip down his. When her face was level with his, he held her for a moment and looked as if he might be going to kiss her, but she stiffened and looked down in confusion, so he let her go the rest of the way, till her feet touched the floor.

There was a moment of complete silence, which Sir Robert broke by saying gruffly, "Those damned things are a menace. Knowing Harry, he probably hasn't kept it up to snuff, either. He'll have to get it looked at and reattached to the rail." He walked over and picked up the ladder which had crashed to the floor, and leaned it against the bookshelves. Her heart still beating furiously, though not from the effects of almost falling, Nicola could say nothing. She turned and ran out of the room.

When her brother found Lady Cynthia in the garden she said, "Well, Robert, did you speak to Miss Fellowes?"

Her brother replied more airily than he felt, "What do you mean, speak to her? I rescued her from falling. The damned library ladder came adrift. Lucky she didn't fall and break her neck."

"What?" They both leaped up. Mr. Prestwick ran into his library, not so much, it must be said, on account of Miss Fellowes, but to make sure all his books were safe.

Lady Cynthia said, "Oh, Robert, that is not how I planned it! I thought if you and Nicola were able to have a few minutes together, you might, you know…."

"I might what?"

"Pop the question, you idiot! The two of you looking like April and May this last week at least. Don't tell me you haven't thought of it!"

"Well, since you bring it up, there was a moment when I was rescuing her that I thought I might, well, kiss her."

"Kiss her! Did she give you any indication she wanted you to kiss her?"

"No, in fact she stiffened and looked away."

"Of course she did! She's a shy, gently-raised woman, not one of your light o' loves! Really, Robert, for a man with your address and success with women, you really don't know us at all! Still," she mused, "it's something to build on, I suppose." She thought again. "I tell you what, don't stay to dinner tonight. Go away. I expect she's regretting not letting you kiss her. She'll be wanting to see you and not see you at the same time. Yes, it may all be for the best. Come back tomorrow. By then, she'll be so glad to see you, she'll fall into your arms."

"Cynthia, you're the most ridiculous woman I know! Fall into my arms indeed! She did fall into them and obviously didn't enjoy the experience. I'm leaving anyway. I'm promised to the Pickfords for dinner. But give Miss Fellowes my regrets that I didn't see her before I left and my hopes she's sustained no injury." He kissed his sister on the cheek and left.

In fact, Nicola's sentiments were exactly what Lady Cynthia described. She kept running over the accident in her mind, at least the part where she slid down Sir Robert's muscular body. She almost cried in frustration that she hadn't let him kiss her. Why was she such a prudish fool? So what if it meant nothing? She would have been kissed by the man she loved and that would have sustained her forever. And as her hostess had said, she experienced equal disappointment and relief when he wasn't at dinner.

Before they went up to bed that evening, Lady Cynthia drew her aside and said, "I'd like to talk to you for a moment, my dear. Irene, why don't you go on up to bed? I won't keep Nicola long."

"I didn't have time to explain before," she said to the governess when they were alone. "It's always such a to-do getting the children ready for bed, though I must say, Irene is a great help. We'll miss her when you have to go." They both sat on the sofa. "I wanted to tell you why Robert didn't stay to dinner. He told me he had been on the point of, well, of kissing you, but you seemed not to welcome his advances. He was both embarrassed and disappointed. That's why he left."

Nicola was stunned. She couldn't believe what she was hearing. He had been disappointed? Could it be true? But why would Lady Cynthia say it if it weren't? She looked at her hostess.

"His advances were not unwelcome," she said quietly, "But I wasn't expecting it and I behaved foolishly. I'm sure you know; I have no experience of that... type of thing." She dashed away the tears that came suddenly to her eyes. "I'm sorry, I...," and she ran out of the room and up the stairs.

Her ladyship remained seated on the sofa a moment, a smile playing around her lips.

The following afternoon when Sir Robert arrived, Miss Fellowes slipped quietly out of the room. This was the opportunity Lady Cynthia needed.

"Just as I said," she told him. "It was only shock that made her react as she did when you looked as if you were going to kiss her.

She was raised strictly and didn't know how to behave. But she loves you. She told me."

Of course, this was not quite true, but her ladyship was determined to have some resolution to this affair.

Before her brother could answer, the knocker sounded and Coombe, the butler, ushered in a woman who looked to be in her mid-thirties, dressed in a pink gown much too young for her. She had several rows of pearls, very obviously glass, around her short neck and hanging down over the front of her plump bosom. She carried a pink parasol with long tassels hanging from the handle. Her bonnet featured a high poke front lined with a pink silk not quite the color of either the parasol or her dress, and embellished with a number of pink and white roses. It might have suited a girl of 18, but looking at her, Lady Cynthia could clearly hear her grandmother's voice: *mutton dressed as lamb, my dear, mutton dressed as lamb*.

"Lady Cynthia," said the lady, coming into the salon with her hand outstretched. "I am Prudence Fullerton. I've come to collect Miss Fellowes and my niece Irene. It is kind of you to have put them up for so long. I hope they've made themselves useful." She looked critically around the salon, which was, as usual, in a disorganized state.

"Indeed they have," responded her ladyship, ignoring the critical glance. "But please let me present my brother, Sir Robert Heathsmith."

Sir Robert, who had been holding back, stepped forward.

Mrs. Fullerton simpered and dipped into a curtsey. "Delighted, I'm sure," she said, holding out her hand, over which he bowed. "La, sir, to think my niece and her governess should have been staying with such society! I hope it don't give them ideas above their station. They'll have to settle down and turn their hand to work in my simple abode. Not that I don't keep a neat place," her eyes swept over the room again, "and a good table." She settled herself on the sofa. "But where are they? Helping with the housework?

"No," said Lady Cynthia more calmly than she felt. "Irene is in the garden with the children and Miss Fellowes is… helping my husband, I believe."

"Let them be brought here so I may give them my instructions," said the newcomer.

Sir Robert raised his eyebrows but went into the hall and spoke quietly to the butler.

In a few minutes Irene appeared with all the children and Molly at her heels. The children ignored the newcomer and began a heated argument as to who would arrange the soldiers for their exercises, who would have the wheeled carriage, who would pull the horse and who would build up the blocks. Since not one of them listened and all strove to be heard, it was bedlam.

Molly, seeing a new friend, bounded up to Mrs. Fullerton and attempted to jump into her lap. The lady shrieked and cried, "Get down you dirty creature! Get down."

Nicola, coming into the room, heard her voice above the din. Sir Robert was delighted to see the elusive dimple peep, though her face immediately became serious.

"SIT DOWN!" said Nicola firmly to Molly, who plumped herself promptly on her wiggling bottom. However, she then performed her new trick of scooting by small degrees, while seated, towards anything or anyone who caught her fancy. In this case it was the pink tassels that hung tantalizingly from the handle of the visitor's parasol.

Miss Fellowes came forward and held out her hand to her would-be employer. Mrs. Fullerton remained seated and touched it with her fingertips.

"Irene," said Nicola, raising her voice to be heard above the children, "I hope you've made your curtsey to your aunt." Irene did.

"Very pretty, I'm sure," said Mrs. Fullerton. "But nice manners won't do you any good if you're not prepared to pitch in."

"Miss Worthington has been very helpful to us with the children since she has been here," interjected Lady Cynthia. In fact, Irene had left the adults and was attempting to sort out the squabbles.

"Good. I shall expect her to watch my youngest. I have recently got rid of Nanny and my six year old needs a firm hand. My older girl will need a governess. Miss Fellowes will take her on."

"But I am employed as Miss Worthington's governess, Madam, she is only 13 and is still a schoolgirl, not a Nanny," said Nicola.

"Oh, at her age, she don't need no more schooling. She'll be much more useful watching out for my Jenny. And I need you for Susan."

Sir Robert's face was becoming more and more grave, and Lady Cynthia had been listening to this exchange with a growing look of astonishment. She was on the point of intervening when Sir Robert stepped forward.

"Forgive me, Mrs. Fullerton," he said in his pleasant voice, "But I think there has been a misunderstanding. There is no question of Miss Fellowes being governess to your daughter. She has just today done me the honor of saying she will become my wife. And I have every intention of applying to Miss Worthington's guardian, her uncle, to allow her to live with us. I am confident he will agree."

There was total silence in the room as Nicola looked at Sir Robert, Mrs. Fullerton looked at Nicola, Lady Cynthia looked at Mrs. Fullerton who had become alarmingly red in the face, and Molly took advantage of the fact that no one at all was looking at her. She could stand it no longer. She leaped up and snapped at the swaying pink tassels. To her own surprise, she caught one and pulled it off, shaking her head from side to side as if she were trying to break the neck of a rat.

Mrs. Fullerton shrieked, stabbing at the puppy with her parasol, "My parasol! My tassels! You wicked, horrible brute!" She stood up and stabbed again, catching the puppy on her side and sending her whimpering under the table.

"Molly!" cried Irene, jumping up from where she was playing with the children, she turned on her aunt. "You awful woman! She's only a puppy and... and your parasol is just... just ugly!" She ran over and knelt down under the table to calm the shaking dog.

Mrs. Fullerton pulled herself up and marched towards the door, her injured parasol in her hand. "I shall leave this... this madhouse," she announced. "I would never have believed members of the nobility could live in such disgraceful disorder: allowing children who should be in the nursery to quarrel disgracefully in front of visitors, sheltering wild animals, and encouraging young women to be disrespectful to their elders and betters. I need not say that neither my niece nor Miss Fellowes will be permitted to cross my threshold. I wish you good day!"

She stamped through the doorway, holding her injured parasol like a sword in front of her, but in the ensuing bedlam, no one paid her any attention. The younger children, who had never heard adults with raised voices, began to cry, and Irene went to comfort them. A revived Molly was being petted by the older twins and was barking with delight. Lady Cynthia burst into laughter. Nicola heard none of it. She ran across the room to Sir Robert, who took her in his arms and kissed her.

"Thank goodness!" said Lady Cynthia. She looked at Nicola, "I take it that's your answer?"

Miss Fellowes looked down and dimpled. Then she raised her eyes with a smile. "Oh, yes," she said. "Yes, yes, yes."

Storming The Citadel

1

"But I don't like him! He's so... so... haughty! And he looks so fierce! He frightens me!" Angela Whiting's large blue eyes filled with tears.

"Don't be silly, Angie," countered Veronica Moreton. "He's not conventionally good-looking, I own, but he's not frightful! I'm sure he's perfectly amiable when you get to know him."

"*You* marry him, then," said her friend with a sob, "I shan't do so. I swear I'll kill myself rather!"

The two friends were sitting in the rather shabby salon of the Whitings' London townhouse, the day after a ball which they had both attended.

"I vow I was ready to drop when Papa told me Lord Jeremy wished to be presented to me. And what other reason can there be than he wants to marry me?"

"There could be all sorts of reasons. You surely don't think every man who's introduced to you wants to marry you?"

"But they do!" wailed her friend. "I am constantly having to refuse offers! You know it's true!"

It *was* true, and looking at her friend, Veronica had to acknowledge it was not surprising. Even with her slightly reddened eyes, Angela was a vision of loveliness, from her white-gold curls to her slender feet. Her big blue eyes shone with innocent appeal, her little nose was perfect and her mouth, with its full pink lips, obviously made for kissing. She was slightly under average height but of such a perfection of figure that no one would have considered her lack of inches a defect. She was shapely but very slender and gave an impression of ethereal fragility. Furthermore, she had a natural reticence that was charming. She was never bold or brash. Her voice was soft and her way of peeping up through her lashes when addressed was entirely without guile. And she was soft-hearted and kind. It genuinely grieved her to have to refuse the many offers of marriage that had already come her way.

Even before they had both left their very excellent Young Ladies' Finishing School in Bath, a number of wholly ineligible suitors had managed to lay their hearts and their hands at Angela's feet, if, thought Veronica with an inward smile, that wasn't a mixed metaphor. From the dancing instructor with the pronounced Adam's apple to the widowed father of one of the younger pupils, Angela had had to rebuff them one and all. Every time, she had come away in tears, her gentle heart touched, even when the offer came from the last person in the world she wished to marry. Yes, thought Veronica, a good fairy had been present at her christening. She was Angela by name and an angel by nature. In fact, this was one of the chief qualities that had drawn her to Angela. She knew her to be genuinely good, whereas she, Veronica, had the unfortunate tendency to laugh at other people's foibles.

"Well, all you have to do is refuse Lord Jeremy, too!" she now replied, "Your Papa will not wish you to marry someone you hold in dislike!"

"You don't know him! He will jump at the chance of my marriage to a man of position and fortune. You can see we need the funds!" She looked around at the faded salon and tears came to her eyes again.

"Take heart," said Veronica. "You never know, he may be the one man in London, or anywhere else, who doesn't wish to marry you. He must have plenty of other opportunities, after all!"

"But how can he? I know he's rich but he's so... ugly. I can't imagine anyone wanting to marry him!"

"He's not ugly! I grant he's not exactly handsome, but he has something else... more interesting."

Veronica herself had found Lord Jeremy Montefort strangely attractive. He was not, as she had said, conventionally good-looking. He had very dark curly hair brushed forward onto his brow, piercing grey eyes, a hooked nose, and Angela was right, a generally haughty air. Although of not more than average height, he was very muscular. The fashion for tight pantaloons could not be said to flatter him, and though his coat fit him well, Veronica had the impression of a powerful force scarcely held in check by the close-fitting superfine and white waistcoat. Altogether he looked a man who knew his own worth. Something about him made her shiver, though she could not say why. He barely glanced at her when Mr. Whiting presented her. He muttered something that was probably *at your service* and gave a perfectly correct bow, but his eyes were already on Angela.

She could not blame him. To say she was a moth to Angela's butterfly was to give less than full credit to the moth. Though she was neither excessively tall nor ill-built, when set next to the ethereal beauty of her friend, with her stockier frame and neat but more generous figure, she looked both. It took a person of unusual perception to admire her dark eyes and abundant hair, and the look of good humor that invariably filled her countenance.

"I don't know why you continue to be bosom-bows with Angela now you are no longer in school, said her Mama to her later that evening. "No gentleman will even look at you so long as you are with Angela. And, really, my dear, while I can't say you're a beauty, you would be good-looking enough to do quite well for yourself if you weren't constantly eclipsed by your friend."

Veronica laughed. "The thing is, Mama, I don't want to do *quite well for myself*. If I ever marry, it will be to a man I love and respect with all my heart, not someone who is *quite* anything! So I don't suppose I ever shall, marry, I mean. A man who would not see me because I was cast into the shade by dear Angela would not do at all," and here she could not stop herself thinking back to Lord Jeremy. "No, he would have to see me for myself, Angela or no Angela. So in fact," she concluded, "being with her is actually saving me a great deal of effort. She acts as a sort of filter."

Her mother sighed, thinking that her daughter did not yet understand the ways of the world. An unmarried woman, unless she was very wealthy, was no one. Or rather, she was a poor someone to fetch and carry for another family member more fortunately placed. But all she said was, "You'd better not tell your father, after all he spent on your coming out."

"I *did* tell you and Papa when you would have it that I be presented," retorted her daughter. "I said it would be the most fearful waste of money and effort. That dress! It cost a fortune, and nothing could have become me less than those white flounces and the feathers in my hair. Why one is forced to dress up like some sort of virginal peacock to be presented at Court is beyond me."

Looking at her daughter, whose animated face was alive with amusement, her dark eyes sparkling, Mrs. Moreton was forced to smile. *There must be someone*, she said to herself, *who will see how pretty and lively she is*, and she sighed.

2

It did not seem to Veronica that at the continual round of parties and routs they attended, Lord Jeremy sought out her friend any more than any of the other pretty women. But if it was a ball or dancing party, he did always come to them near the beginning, when their dance cards were still unfilled. Angela would clutch her hand whenever he approached and it would be Veronica who greeted him cheerfully and exchanged a few words, until her friend had the courage to peep up between her lashes and quietly answer his salutations. He very properly asked her to dance after he had escorted Angela once onto the floor. He was a wonderful dancer, and it seemed a lucky coincidence to Veronica that she usually ended up doing a waltz with him.

"Thank goodness he didn't ask me to waltz again!" whispered Angela. "You know that time he asked me, he made me so terribly nervous, I stepped on his feet. His hand on my back was so *warm* and *strong* somehow. I felt powerless." She shuddered.

Since these were precisely the qualities that Veronica enjoyed, she gave no answer to this confession. She loved to dance, and with the slight pressure of that warm, firm hand on her back, she felt she was flying around the floor.

Other than the usual polite enquiries into her health, his lordship did not at first converse a great deal while dancing, but on one occasion he must have felt her giggle under her breath, for he asked, "What do you find so amusing, Miss Moreton?"

She could have answered that in general she found a great deal that made her laugh, for she had a fine sense of the ridiculous, but she just said, "The Earl of Westchester, over there. Surely everyone must be amused by his antics!"

The gentleman in question was not content with taking his partner onto the floor in the usual fashion. Before beginning the dance, he had the habit of performing a very elaborate bow, twirling his hand in the air above his head before thrusting his leg forward and bowing so low his nose almost touched his knee, like a nobleman in the Court of Louis XIV, if the tales of that extravagant time were to be believed.

"Oh, old Bernie! Yes, he does like to make a show," replied her partner. "I suppose we're all used to him and pay him no mind."

"It makes me laugh every time I see it," confessed Veronica. "He once led me onto the floor and performed the same gyrations. I thought at first he was making a joke, and I nearly laughed out loud. Then I saw he was serious. I had to struggle to keep a straight face. I don't know if he realized it. He's never asked me to dance again."

"Oh, I doubt he realized it. He is so sure of his own glory it would be inconceivable to him that anyone should find him an object of amusement," smiled Lord Jeremy.

"I'm glad to hear it. I know he only asked me in the first place because, having solicited Miss Whiting, he felt duty bound to ask me, too. I get a lot of partners that way." She laughed gaily.

He made no response, which did not surprise Veronica because she thought that was precisely what he had done himself.

After that, he would often ask her what she found amusing, and she would regale him with whatever had caught her fancy. On one occasion, Lady Summers had brought her lapdog to a soirée, under the illusion that no one could see his little head poking out from her well-developed bosom. Since that part of her body was also festooned in at least three strings of pearls (glass!), a large corsage of paper violets and a hideous brooch the size of a saucer, encrusted with a mountain of colored stones of dubious authenticity, the animal was well camouflaged. Indeed, Lord Jeremy had not noticed it until Veronica pointed it out. Then he laughed out loud when she said she was tempted to dangle a sweetmeat in front of the little dog to see if he would leap from his hiding place, rather like Minerva being born from the head of Zeus. She noticed for the first time how his face was transformed when he smiled.

"What were you and Lord Jeremy laughing about?" asked Angela, coming back to where Veronica was sitting.

"About Minerva being born from the head of Zeus," replied her friend dwelling on the memory of that smile. "He was no doubt waiting for you to return, but you were so long, he just left."

"That seems an odd thing to laugh about!"

"Well, I was telling him about the dog in Lady Summers' bosom. He hadn't noticed it."

Her friend looked at her strangely, wondering what Zeus and Minerva had to do with the dog, which she had noticed. But the thought was soon chased from her mind by a more interesting discussion of the new style of sleeves on Mrs. Winthrop's gown.

About this time a newcomer appeared on the scene. He was a beautiful young man with a face and figure that would not have been out of place on a statue. He could have modelled for Apollo. His fair hair curled away from a noble brow, his nose was manly and straight, his chin firm in a square jaw and his lips neither too thin nor too full. He was the younger son of a fine old family, just down from Oxford and studying for the Church.

Evander Carleton was immediately a great favorite with all the unwed maidens, though not so much with their Mamas and Papas, since his fortune was known to be limited. The girls clustered around him like the proverbial bees, and it was soon reported that he was absolutely charming. Indeed, he was. He was accustomed to being courted, but this had not made him vain or demanding. He was as happy to sit discussing the glories of a walk in the park with one of the beauties of the season as he was talking about the latest play he simply *must* see with one of her less well-favored friends. He was a graceful dancer. The ladies adored him. Nor was he lacking in manly attributes. He was shown to be a capital whip; his greys, which he handled with finesse, were deemed excellent cattle but not showy. He played a good hand of cards and smiled as much when he lost as when he won. The gentlemen, too, thought him a fine fellow.

It was not long before he found Angela. To see them sitting together, both divinely fair and perfect in face and physique, was to catch a glimpse of some paradise where the celestial beings were far above all mortal men. The other men found it prudent not to approach Angela when Evander was sitting with her. They could compete with neither his beauty nor his conversation, and Angela, who generally sat with her head lowered when in the company of the opposite sex, lifted her eyes to his countenance, where they remained, entranced.

Veronica found it all very amusing. To watch the crestfallen faces of the other young men who, making their way towards their angel, found themselves pipped to the post by Evander and then, to continue the metaphor (really, thought Veronica, she must stop thinking in such terms), standing by the side of the track waiting for a stretch of open field, was in itself a sport. She knew nothing of handicapping, but if she had, it was sure she would have found that very good fun.

The one man who seemed entirely unconcerned by the new arrival was Lord Jeremy. Sooner or later he would saunter over in his characteristic way, make his bow, and sit down. He would attempt to engage the whole group in conversation but before long be forced to give up, when it became clear the celestial beings only had eyes for each other. He would then turn his attention to Veronica, and more often than not utter a comment that would make her laugh.

"I see the citadel has been stormed by superior forces," he remarked, "but the infidels are outside the gates, awaiting their chance."

"How funny!" she said, looking around at the hovering suitors. "I was thinking of it more in terms of a horse race, but whether they are infidels or inferior jockeys, I think they stand no chance."

She wondered how he would take that, since surely he himself was one of the group, however one named them, that they stood no chance. But he agreed laughingly and turned the conversation to something else.

3

Since childhood, Veronica had been subject to occasional debilitating earaches. They had become less frequent as she had grown, but the pain was no less severe. A few days later, she woke up in the early morning with such pain in her ear that she nearly cried. She stumbled down to the kitchen and with the help of one of the maids, found an onion that was put on to boil. This was an ancient remedy one of the mistresses at school had taught her. One boiled an onion until soft, let it cool until it could be comfortably handled and then placed it against the ear canal. By gentle squeezing, the center of the onion, still warmer than the outside, entered the orifice. It would then be held against the ear by a tightly bound scarf. If she then took a sip of laudanum, she found she could sleep. When she awoke, the pain would be significantly less, and it usually wore off completely within a day.

The remedy worked as it usually did, and by the afternoon she was feeling much better. Not better enough, however, to attend Lady Peckwith's rout that evening. She sent a note of excuse to her ladyship, and another to Angela. Within the hour her friend was at her side.

"I shall stay with you this evening and not go to the rout," she declared. "I could not be easy knowing you were suffering."

This was said with absolute sincerity, and Veronica thought again how kind her friend was. She knew she was dying to see Evander, with whom she could only meet in public places and whom she hadn't seen in nearly a week.

"You goose!" she said fondly to Angela. "I'm not suffering. In fact, if I go to sleep early, I daresay the pain will be gone entirely when I awake. You go to the rout and see Evander. You know you want to!"

"Not more than I want to stay with my dear friend in her hour of need!"

Veronica laughed. "Now you sound like the heroine of one of Mrs. Radcliffe's novels! Please, Angela, don't worry about me. I shall do famously! Besides I want you to go so you can tell me all the sights I missed. You can be my ears and eyes. Please go, dear."

"If you're really sure?"

"I am! I promise! Now off you go and make yourself beautiful... or more beautiful, if you can!"

Angela left, promising to tell her all about it on the morrow.

But before eleven the next morning, the knocker sounded and the butler took delivery of a huge basket of flowers. He took it in to Miss Moreton, who was sitting on the sofa, looking much better, but with her head still wrapped in a shawl. The attached note read:

Dear Miss Moreton,

> *I was sorry to hear of your indisposition. You'll not be surprised to learn that not one of the infidels was able to storm the citadel. I kept watch on your behalf.*

Yours etc.,
Montefort

Veronica laughed out loud and was still smiling when Angela was shown into the room. One look at her, however, wiped all the smile from her face.

"Angela, whatever is the matter?" she cried.

"He wants to marry me!" wailed her friend.

"Who?" Veronica was conscious of a sinking feeling in the pit of her stomach. "Lord Jeremy?"

"No, Evander!" She burst into tears.

Accustomed to her friend's frequent tears, Veronica let her cry herself out, simply patting her back and uttering shushing sounds. At length, Angela wiped her tears with a scrap of lace from her reticule and shuddering, lifted her head.

"Evander asked me to become his wife and oh, Veronica! I want to, I do! But I know my father will never permit it as long as there's a chance Lord Jeremy might declare himself. Last night he sat with Evander and me nearly all evening, saying practically nothing. You know how he is, at least, you're the only person he actually talks to, as far as I can tell. Then he said he could see I was thirsty—and indeed I was, it was frightfully hot in there and I was fanning myself like a madwoman—and went to procure me a lemonade. That's when Evander had a chance to ask me."

"It was nice of him to bring you a lemonade. I suppose Evander didn't think of it?"

"How could he? He wanted to ask me to marry him! His mind wasn't on lemonade!" Angela sounded almost affronted.

In spite of herself, Veronica almost smiled at the idea that a man was so fixed on one idea he couldn't see his beloved was in urgent need of refreshment.

"So how did you answer?"

"I said I would marry him with all my heart, but Papa will never agree. He thinks Lord Jeremy is on the point of declaring himself, because he comes and sits with us at every opportunity. Evander has a little family money and when he gets a living, which, he says, he's sure to do, there will be enough for us to live comfortably. But it's not enough to satisfy Papa, compared with Lord Jeremy!"

"But I'm sure he would not compel you to marry one man when you are in love with another! Your Papa is not such a monster."

"I know, but I couldn't make him… vexed with me." Tears filled Angela's eyes again.

That was probably true, thought Veronica. Her friend was completely unused to anyone being angry with her. For who could be cross with an angel?

Suddenly, Angela sat up and looked at her.

"Veronica," she said breathlessly, "you can talk to Lord Jeremy! He likes talking to you. Will you go and tell him please to stop paying me his attentions. To never come near me again. Papa will see he's not going to propose. Then if Evander goes to ask him for my hand, he's bound to agree. No one could refuse Evander anything!"

Once again, Veronica was forced to agree. Who could refuse a man who looked like Apollo? But ask Lord Jeremy to stop paying court to Angela? She couldn't! Every feeling revolted!

"Talk to Lord Jeremy? No, Angela! I couldn't do that!"

"Why not? You always talk to him! You and he laugh together! He likes you!"

"He talks to me because you're generally tongue-tied in his presence! He doesn't like me! What nonsense!"

"But Veronica! It's such a little thing. All you have to do is tell him I'm in love with Evander and to please stay away from me. My whole future happiness depends upon it!"

Veronica experienced a pang thinking how much her enjoyment of everything would be undermined if Lord Jeremy stayed away. But then she thought, here was her chance to do something for her friend, who would certainly do the same for her. When they were at school Angela always acted as her protectress, taking blame upon herself anytime Veronica's too ready tongue got her in trouble. She always said Veronica was only repeating what she had said. No one ever believed it, of course, but the teachers were always bewitched by Angela and let it go. She sighed.

"Very well, I'll go and speak to him. If you never see me again, send the Bow Street Runners to look for my bones!"

She laughed ruefully, but Angela just looked horrified.

Two days later, Veronica descended from the carriage outside the Montefort townhome. It was an imposing building with wide double doors and a white stucco portico. Her maid trod the front steps behind her and when they gained entry, Veronica bade her sit in the hall while she was led into the presence of Lord Jeremy.

He was standing by the fireplace in the salon and came forward to greet her. The room was as unlike its owner as could be imagined. Where he was dark, muscular, and often frowning, it was light-filled and pleasant. The walls were a pale blue with a white frieze and fireplace. A large pale colored rug lay on the floor, with a central medallion in blues and greens. The Queen Anne style furniture with its curving shapes looked elegant and comfortable. Opposite the fireplace was a sofa with straw-colored cushioned seats. On either side of the fireplace were two blue velvet wing-back chairs, and against the wall stood a large secretary desk-bookcase. On the walls were light-colored watercolor scenes, and over the fireplace a large gold-framed mirror. Only her breeding kept Veronica from exclaiming, *What a lovely room!*

"Miss Moreton," said her host, holding out his hand. "This is an unexpected pleasure! I'm so pleased to see you recovered from your recent indisposition. Do sit down." He led her to the sofa, then went to one of the wing chairs. "How may I be of service to you?"

Now she was here, Veronica was for once bereft of words. She didn't know where to begin and started somewhere safe.

"Thank you for the lovely flowers. They cheered me immensely and are still doing so."

"I'm glad you liked them. I missed you at Lady Peckwith's. I had no one to laugh with." He smiled and his face was transformed. Suddenly he didn't seem so at odds with the light-filled room.

"The thing is, my lord...," she began again.

"Call me Jeremy," he interrupted.

Veronica felt herself blush, something she couldn't remember ever doing before.

"Oh, I don't think…."

"Of course you can. We are alone. You may call me anything."

She took a deep breath. "The thing is… Jeremy, Angela has asked me to speak to you."

His face fell. "Oh, I see."

Veronica said, all in a rush, "She has asked me to beg you to stop paying her your addresses. She's in love with Evander and her Papa won't agree to their marriage if you are still in the picture."

There was complete silence.

Then Lord Jeremy said slowly, "I am to discontinue my addresses to Miss Whiting because her father won't let her marry Carleton if I'm still *in the picture*." He gave the last words a special emphasis. Then he looked straight at her. "Tell me, Miss Moreton, what has given you, or anyone, the impression I am paying my addresses to Miss Whiting? As far as I remember, she practically refuses to look me in the face, stumbles over my feet when we dance and answers any question I put to her in the shortest monosyllables."

"But… but, I just assumed… we both just assumed…."

"Let me put Miss Whiting's mind at rest. I have no intention of proposing marriage to her. My intentions lie in quite another direction."

Veronica was astonished. Then she didn't know whether to be happy or miserable. "In quite another direction?" she gulped.

"Yes. I suppose you're going to tell me that's impossible. Your friend Angela is every man's choice. A pearl beyond price, a diamond of the first water, a piece of perfection in nature," and as she seemed on the point of agreeing, he quickly added, "but let me tell you, Miss Moreton, I quickly found that a pearl does not laugh, a diamond does not dance, and a piece of perfection is a dead bore. Now, if you would, tell me who smiles at me constantly, makes me laugh, does not stumble over my feet and makes the most unlikely comparisons between a lapdog in a dowager's bosom to Minerva emerging from the head of Zeus?"

Veronica looked at him, a smile playing on her lips. "Well, that would be me, or I, grammatically speaking."

Lord Jeremy stood up and took two long strides towards her. "Yes it would, grammar be damned. Stand up please, Miss Moreton."

Her heart pounding, Veronica did as she was bid. Lord Jeremy took her fiercely in his arms. "Will you marry me, Miss Moreton?"

She looked up at him and smiled. "Do you have a generous living for a clergyman in your gift?"

"Yes, I believe I do," he said.

"Will you go and tell Mr. Whiting there's no chance of your marrying his daughter and he'd better take the clergyman to whom this generous living is to be offered?"

"If I must."

"You must. And will you call me Veronica instead of Miss Moreton?"

"Certainly."

"In that case, yes, Jeremy, I will."

"You're a generous woman, Veronica. You could have asked me anything for yourself and I would have said yes."

"I know. But Angela is my friend and I desire her happiness as much as my own. But there is one thing I want from you."

"You have but to name it."

"Kiss me, Jeremy," she said.

"Your most obedient," he said, and he did.

The End

A Note from the Author

If you enjoyed this novel, please leave a review! Go to the Amazon page and scroll down past all the other books Amazon wants you to buy(!) till you get to the review click. Thank you so much!

For a free short story and to listen to the author read the first chapter of all her novels, please go to the website:

https://romancenovelsbyglrobinson.com

An Excerpt from *Héloise Says No*

Chapter One

"Thank you for your flattering attention, my lord, but the answer is *no*."

So saying, Mrs. Héloise Ramsay curtseyed and left. Rory Compton, third Earl of Dexter and one of the most sought-after men in London, watched her go, anger narrowing his lips. Even so, he couldn't help admiring her shapely derrière as she crossed the room away from him. It was more than usually revealed because she had looped up the train of her ballgown onto her wrist and the shimmering overdress pulled at the silk beneath. To his mind, she was the most fascinating woman in London. Not as young as the girls in their first season, of course. He estimated she must be over twenty, but she was so very much more alluring than any of those damsels.

Lord Dexter was by then in his thirtieth year and even he would have agreed he'd been spoiled all his life. He had been born with the proverbial silver spoon in his mouth and with his good looks and charm had always been able to have his own way. His nanny had adored him, his tutors had been unable to reprimand him, he had been popular at school, both for his sporting ability and his open-handedness, and had sailed through Oxford with the minimum of effort and the maximum of charm.

His father was one of the Prince's cronies, both before and in the early days of his Regency, and followed him everywhere, with the result that as a boy, Rory saw him only rarely. He was therefore only dutifully fond of him and when he conveniently died during Rory's twenty-eighth year, he had not mourned his loss overlong. He had assumed the title and the fortune that went with it.

The only way this had materially affected his life was that his mother, whom he genuinely loved, had wanted to remove to a pleasant house overlooking one of the small parks for which London was well known. She had come to dislike the Dexter townhome with its large, cold rooms, filled with her husband's noisy and often intoxicated cronies. Rory had taken possession of it, as happy to be there as in his rather luxurious lodgings. Like everything else he owned, he let others run it. He occasionally met with his housekeeper, his agent, and his man of business, agreed with everything they said and left them, once again victims of his charm, to do whatever they saw fit.

He had been the darling of the *ton* ten seasons, though the mothers of hopeful maidens thrust into the marriage mart every year had long since given up on him. He was simply not interested in those young damsels, and indeed, never had been, even when younger himself.

He was well known to be rich enough, as the saying went, to buy an abbey, but preferred to spend his blunt on his stable. He was an expert rider, both in the hunt and with his racing curricle and pair, with which he regularly beat all-comers. Added to that, he was a good shot and a frequent visitor to Manton's shooting gallery on Davies Street. He was well known to be able to hit twelve wafers from a distance of fifteen yards in under the six minutes declared necessary for an expert. As a consequence, he was very rarely challenged to a duel, even when the wives of important gentlemen smiled a little too fondly at him.

He was popular in the Clubs, open handed at the card table, as good humored when he lost as when he won. He was a good dancer and never let his hostess down by playing cards all night and leaving partnerless females to sit in the corner all night.

But he seemed to have no interest at all in forming a permanent connection with any woman, or any connection at all with a young lady. For a month or two he would be seen with one or another lovely widow on his arm. Then she would appear with an expensive parure of jewelry and another would take her place. Mrs. Ramsay's refusal was the first check he had met with in his life.

She had appeared on the scene the year before, introduced by, of all people, Lady Pevensey, a very high flyer indeed. She had been presented as *the daughter of a friend of the family*, and such was her ladyship's unassailable position in the *ton* that no one had questioned who that friend might be, or where her daughter had come from.

It was all the more astonishing then, when it became apparent that Mrs. Ramsay was for temporary sale to anyone who would meet her price.

The first of these had been young Brownlow, just out of Cambridge and sowing some very wild oats indeed. For three months she graced his arm at the opera, at parties and anywhere the young and fashionable might go to see and be seen.

To be sure, she never entered the salons of Almack's, but whether that was because she chose not to go there or had been refused vouchers by the patronesses, no one ever knew. It was whispered behind more than one fan that it was unlikely even those ladies, so full of their own importance, would have dared refuse someone championed by Lady Pevensey. It was more probable Mrs. Ramsay herself had decided to avoid the venue. But she never said, and they dared not ask.

For the following three months Lionel Cartaret had been the lucky fellow to squire her. If Brownlow was young, Cartaret was, frankly, old. The *ton* was amazed when he took up with the lady. His wife had been dead these fifteen years and in that time he had never shown any interest in a possible replacement. Yet there he was, his somewhat bent back and bald head held perceptibly straighter as he accompanied the lovely lady everywhere. It had to be said, she treated him no differently from how she had treated Brownlow. She smiled kindly at him, spoke in an undertone, never embarrassed him by laughing too loud, playing roguishly with her fan or in any way acting otherwise than with perfect decorum.

Courtesan she might be, but it was very hard to dislike her. She was polite, self-effacing, and kind. She was as likely to spend half an hour talking to an ignored debutante in the corner as a wealthy peer. And even her few detractors had to admit she had a perfection of figure it was impossible to deny, and a face that held one's attention. Neither owed anything to artifice. She employed neither powder nor paint, nor, as far as one could tell, any corset, though she was very shapely, as Lord Dexter had once again irritably witnessed.

She had light brown curls unremarkable except for their abundance, and calm grey eyes fringed by very dark lashes. She was of average height, but her carriage made her appear taller, taller in fact, than the elderly Lord Cartaret. She dressed quietly but with elegance, danced gracefully, and when addressed spoke in pleasant tones, giving her interlocutor her whole attention without hesitation or coquetry.

If one examined her closely, as Lord Dexter had, one could often perceive the light of humor in her wide eyes, and her mouth had a tendency to curl up at the edges as if she were about to smile. Taken separately, nothing about her was truly remarkable, taken together, however, she really was quite irresistible. Lord Dexter had found it almost impossible, these last months, to take his eyes off her.

He was pipped at the post, however, when, at the end of three months with Cartaret, she appeared with Greville. Bryce Greville was a man of about his lordship's age. He had never married, nor, indeed seemed interested in women. He was a tall, thin, bookish fellow who, it was reported, studied the flora and fauna of his native Kent and was happier in a field than in the London salons. It was certainly true that for the period of her involvement with him, Mrs. Ramsay was often absent from the tonnish events of the season. But now, three months later, seeing her alone at the ball, Lord Dexter had thought it might be time to make his interest known.

If you want to find out how the story of Lord Dexter and the lovely Héloïse Ramsey progresses, please go to:

https://www.amazon.com/gp/product/B09RPYCYZS

Other Regency Novels by GL Robinson

My Amazon Author Pages: GLRobinson-US   GLRobinson-UK

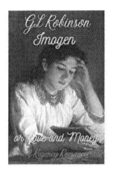

Imogen or Love and Money Lovely young widow Imogen is pursued by Lord Ivo, a well-known rake. She angrily rejects him and concentrates on continuing her late husband's business enterprises. But will she find that money is more important than love?

Cecilia or Too Tall to Love Orphaned Cecilia, too tall and too outspoken for acceptance by the *ton,* is determined to open a school for girls in London's East End slums, but is lacking funds. When Lord Tommy Allenby offers her a way out, will she get more than she bargained for?

Rosemary or Too Clever to Love Governess Rosemary is forced to move with her pupil, the romantically-minded Marianne, to live with the girl's guardian, a strict gentleman with old fashioned ideas about young women should behave. Can she save the one from her own folly and persuade the other that she isn't just a not-so-pretty face?

The Kissing Ball A collection of Regency short stories, not just for Christmas. All sorts of seasons and reasons!

The Earl and The Mud-Covered Maiden *The House of Hale Book One*. When a handsome stranger covers her in mud driving too fast and then lies about his name, little does Sophy know her world is about to change forever.

The Earl and His Lady *The House of Hale Book Two*. Sophy and Lysander are married, but she is unused to London society and he's very proud of his family name. It's a rocky beginning for both of them.

The Earl and The Heir *The House of Hale Book Three*. The Hale family has a new heir, in the shape of Sylvester, a handful of a little boy with a lively curiosity. His mother is curious too, about her husband's past. They both get themselves in a lot of trouble.

The Lord and the Red-Headed Hornet Orphaned Amelia talks her way into a man's job as secretary to a member of the aristocracy. She's looking for a post in the Diplomatic Service for her twin brother. But he wants to join the army. And her boss goes missing on the day he is supposed to show up for a wager. Can feisty Amelia save them both?

The Lord and the Cat's Meow A love tangle between a Lord, a retired Colonel, a lovely debutante, and a fierce animal rights activist. But Horace the cat knows what he wants. He sorts it out.

The Lord and the Bluestocking The Marquess of Hastings is good-looking and rich but is a little odd. Nowadays he would probably be diagnosed as having Asperger's syndrome. To find a wife he scandalizes the ton by advertising in the newspaper. Elisabeth Maxwell is having no luck finding a publisher for her children's book and is willing to marry him to escape an overbearing step-father. This gently amusing story introduces us to an unusual but endearing Regency couple. The question is: can they possibly co-exist, let alone find happiness?

About The Author

GL Robinson is a retired French professor who took to writing Regency Romances in 2018. She dedicates all her books to her sister, who died unexpectedly that year and who, like her, had a lifelong love of the genre. She remembers the two of them reading Georgette Heyer after lights out under the covers in their convent boarding school and giggling together in delicious complicity.

Brought up in the south of England, she has spent the last forty years in upstate New York with her American husband. She likes gardening, talking with her grandchildren and sitting by the fire. She still reads Georgette Heyer.

Made in the USA
Columbia, SC
04 December 2024